# 19TH AND UNIVERSITY

# The Austintacious Quartet

*Ostentatious but gracious*

BOOK I

# 19<sup>TH</sup> AND UNIVERSITY
## A tale of 1968 Austin

by
l.k. siga & Barbara Light Lacy

Rising Times Books
A Division of Golightly Publishing

ISBN13:  978-0-9617721-4-7 (paperback)
ISBN13:  978-0-9617721-6-1 (Amazon Kindle)
ISBN13:  978-0-9617721-5-4 (ePub)

Published in the United States by Rising Times Books, A division of Golightly Publishing
P O Bos 181533
Dallas, Texas 75218-1533

Visit our website at www.risingtimesbooks.com.

Publisher's Cataloging-in-Publication Data
1. Nineteen sixties – Fiction.  2.  Austin (Tex.) – Fiction.  3.  University of Texas at Austin – Fiction.  4.  Counterculture – Fiction.  5.  Hippies – Fiction.

I. Title. II. A tale of 1968 Austin

L.K. Siga; Barbara Light Lacy

Cover Design by Helen Granger/High Road Marketing and Communications

For information about permission to reproduce selections from this book, write to Permissions, Golightly Publishing, P. O. Box 181533, Dallas, Texas 75218-1533 or email contact@risingtimesbooks.com

First Edition:  April 2012.
10 9 8 7 6 5 4 3 2 1

# CHAPTER ONE

*Tres came to Jack first and said, "The* Austin Chronicle *and the* Austin American Statesman *like to say how cool the '60s were and how you guys were doing things that didn't even have a name yet and, well, since you and Gram were there …?"*

*"Oh hell yeah we were there."*

*"So what was Austin was like back then?"*

*"It was cool. At least it sure seems that way now. For one thing there was a lot less traffic. You could get anywhere in town in fifteen minutes." Jack chuckled and said, "The truth is, I halfway didn't want to go to Austin but my granpa wouldn't quit wartin' me about it an' nobody gets to you like your family."*

*"So start there," Tres said, "start when your granpa made you come to Austin."*

*"It was South Brewster County. Northern Chihuahua Desert badlands. Rancho Quien Sabe. A mile south of Terlingua. Down along the Rio Grande."*

. . .

The '60s were set in motion for Jack on the front porch of Rancho Quien Sabe's adobe structure on a September evening in 1965. Rancho Quien Sabe was "the home place," where Jack had spent all the life he could remember.

Though Jack and Grandpa Gage were on the porch just as they had been countless evenings before, tonight was different. Sure, the sunset was beautiful and the view breathtaking with the mouth of Santa Elena Canyon a mile away and Big Bend National Park five miles to the east, its blue-tinted Chisos "Ghost" Mountains in full view from Mule Ears Peaks to Emory Peak to Casa Grande and stretching on a northeasterly line for fifty miles. By now the southwest wind had become a light breeze, a million stars had begun to dot the colossal black sky and the Chihuahua Desert's night life was rousing itself. Mr. Bullsnake had come out from under the adobe structure's rock foundation to slither through the adobe's living fence of ocotillo stalks then on down through the candelilla, sotol, creosote and greasewood to the outhouse that Jack thought had just about the best view anywhere. On the edge of darkness quail were calling to one other, a cottontail was nibbling lechugilla and a roadrunner was hunting bugs. Two hundred yards to the south the Rio Grande was running as steady and true as time itself and this was where Nacho—Jack's other grandfather, the daddy of Jack's mother—was waiting with two burros on a sand bank by the Texas side of the Rio Grande. Nacho was serenading the burros with a wood flute while keeping an eye on the great maw to his right that was Santa Elena Canyon's exit, its 800-foot-high walls a hundred yards wide and making what Jack, ever since he was little, saw as a door to the sky.

Meanwhile, though the old man and the young one were supposedly keeping an eye on Nacho, they were distracted by what Nacho's Maya culture called *xutan:* feeling a change before it happened. The change that was coming was a done deal that had been planned for years by Granpa and Nacho: Jack was going off to college.

Jack sat on the flat white river rock that served as the front stoop for the adobe's dilapidated porch. He was idly picking and strumming his Mexican six string guitar while watching a nearby horned toad use the twilight to dine on red ants. Like the small adobe home it fronted, there was not much to the porch. It had no

2

floorboards, only built-up creek sand cemented by the few and far between rains and packed down by the boots of whoever had come by to sit a spell since the summer of 1951, when Granpa and Nacho had brought their grandson Jack here, just after the boy's parents had been killed in a car wreck on U.S. Highway 67 south of Fort Stockton. The porch's shed roof, save for a piece of rusting, bent-by-the-wind rectangle of corrugated tin that a blue norther had left behind a few years back, was made of ocotillo branches and, like the piece of tin, nailed to weathered gray two-by-fours above the screen door that let you into the adobe.

Granpa himself was in the bentwood rocker that Nacho had brought up from Mexico. Next to his Nocona boots were piles of long outdated *Saturday Evening Post* and *Time* magazines and *Big Bend Sentinels*. He was whittling a piece of mesquite with a Case pocket knife Jack had given him last Christmas. Whittling was pretty much all he did anymore, this evening's piece of mesquite destined to be a slingshot stock. Both Granpa and Jack wore jeans and, like their black Nocona boots, those jeans were so well broken in that Granpa liked to joke they practically put themselves on. Jack had on a plain white T-shirt, Granpa a long sleeved Khaki shirt—how they had dressed every day of their lives unless there was a funeral to attend. Between Granpa's legs was a bottle of Senor Fuego tequila. In the porch's southwest corner Nacho's red, yellow and blue cotton hammock swayed on and off in the breeze.

As soon as Granpa Gage tossed the finished slingshot stock beside his grandson Jack picked it up and said, "Much obliged, Granpa, I'll add it to my collection." Then, with a teasing smile: "You know, Scooter Culero calls slingshots by a different name."

"Don't surprise me none."

"Scooter signed up, Granpa. Says he's gonna be a marine."

"Don't sound like Scooter—no women in the marines…not yet anyhow."

"Scooter says he's got a plan."

"Good for Scooter. But you gotta a better plan, Ben Jack. Signin' up to go to the University of Texas is a right mite smarter than

3

signin' up for a deal where they play for keeps, mebbe git yoreself kilt in a foreign land nobody never heard of nor even knows where it's at."

Jack just grinned and began to wonder as he had all his life why those Chisos Mountains were blue when he heard his granpa say:

"Ya know you're the first one in this family to go off to college, don't ya?"

"Yessir, I do…but I'm yet to be certain if that's a good thing or a bad thing."

"Like Nacho says, 'time'll tell.'" Then cleared his throat, spat and said, "You all packed? Ready to go for a spin?"

"Yessir, I believe I am."

"You got grub for the highway?"

"Yessir. Nacho fixed up some Tamale Pie, also some of his asparagus rolls."

"Is that consarned contraption you call the Fitty Six gassed up? Tires kicked?"

"The tires're good. I'll fill er up in Marathon. It's only 37 cents a gallon there."

"Dadblamed price of gasoline's gone sky high."

Jack said nothing. He was wondering if the gas pump jockey in Marathon would take the white plastic Jesus Nacho had glued to the Fitty Six's dashboard.

Grinning now, Granpa said, "You be sure'n mind that new paint job on the Fitty Six 'cause it means a lot to ol' Nacho." Then: "Only a Mexican would put nine coats of baby spit yellow lacquer on a pickup."

Jack shook his head. "Nacho didn't even ask, just went ahead'n did it."

"He said he did it so you'd look prosperous to the pincharitas."

"Back when I was at Boys State I saw one in the lobby of the Texas Theatre an' I'm here to tell you she sure was some kind of special beautiful, yes, she was."

The old man jabbed his Case pocketknife toward Jack and said, "Boy, you listen here when I say that you'd best watch out for

4

pincharitas. One'll set her hook in you an' afore you can come un-cross-eyed she'll be putting the splice on ya—an' I'm here to tellya that's the worse goldang trap ya ever saw."

"Yessir."

"What about *Analuz*? She all set?"

"Yessir. Everthing's good to go. I'll head out soon as Nacho's done."

"When ya git ta Austin," Granpa said, "go down to the river—it'll be good for you'n *Analuz*."

"Yessir. I can't wait."

"Ya got plenty of money in case ya break down 'tween here an' there?"

"Yessir, I believe I got it covered."

"Now tell me again what kinda place J. Frank got you."

"Mr. Dobie passed away last year, Granpa."

"Durn, I plumb forgot. Guess I'm livin' in the past. That an' I gotta twinge of the misery from the hooch. Lumbago's ailing me too an' could be my sacroiliac's goin' out...so where are ya gonna live in Austin?"

"With Michael A. and Aunt Sofi."

"Been known to happen that places change folks, Ben Jack. Just be respectful an' don't judge their ways nor their home place 'cause ever place is home ta somebody. We've always run a cold camp around here so you'll find that city life's different—but don't let them city folks take advantage, ya hear?"

"Yessir."

"How much is the rent gonna run ya?"

"Twenty-five dollars a month."

"Lawsy mercy! That don't sound like no family rate ta me. That's flat out a lotta money. A feller goin' to college at Sul Ross up in Alpine could rent hisself a whole house for that amount of *dinero*. An' how much was it you said the tuition's gonna be over there in Austin?"

"Fifty dollars a semester plus books and fees."

"Pure D highway robbery! Dadblamed, lamebrained, mule-mouthed politicians."

"Yessir. Mule-mouthed politicians talking out of both sides of their mouth." Next Jack got a teasing grin on his face and said, "I'd appreciate it if ya'd tell me one more time about bein' in the Rangers with Sul Ross."

"Awww, ol' Sully was afore my time and you know it, Mr. Smart Aleck. Was J. Frank an' me come out here to the Big Empty on the train in, oh, 1917 or '18 I think it was, J. Frank ta teach school—"

"It was 1910 when Mr. Dobie taught school in Alpine, Granpa."

"1910?...mighta been, I don't recollect as good as I use ta... had me a time though Rangerin' an' puttin' a stop to Pancho Villa crossin' the border an' gettin' the local pincharitas to pat out tortillas for him'n his boys. Later on, J. Frank chucked it in an' ended up in Austin, made himself a famous folklore perfesser, wrote books whut told how Texas was back then. Me, well, sometimes ya gotta go along to get along so I married your Granma an' stuck with Rangerin' just long enough to get your daddy borned and growed up with a good size on him—not that I got doodly for a pension, just that pair of Lucchese boots I give ya, what Governor Ma Ferguson give us Rangers for protectin' the border...then"—voice sadder in tone—"your Daddy and Momma died in the wreck what orphaned you an' eventually, even though she was a tough ol' bird, was the grief whut kilt your Granma. That was when Nacho said he had this little piece of land called 'Rancho Quien Sabe' an' I oughta come on down here an' we'd raise you an' go fishin.'"

"There aren't any fish in that river, Granpa."

"I know it! That ain't the point, never was. Boy, if you don't beat all I ever saw—you always were a smart aleck kid. Ya oughta get along just fine in Austin with all them other smart aleck kids, them teasips." The old man paused before saying, "Anyhow , as I was sayin' 'fore I was so rudely interrupted, me'n Nacho fixed up the Rancho Quien Sabe just enough to let us be a fine pair of nature's layabouts. Course lately Nacho's been pullin' purt near all the weight."

"Nacho says I should visit Mayaluum someday—what do you think?"

"Go ahead on. It's a pure D powerful place to see and know."

"You mean that?"

"Yes indeedy. A trip down there'd do anybody justice. Nacho's a Maya daykeeper an' him an' his people got thousands of years of culture on their side. I've come to believe that they flat out know where the center of the Earth is."

"Like he says, 'Look to the past for lessons and the future for answers.'"

The old man sighed and said, "You think we about covered everthin'?"

"Just about, yessir."

"What'd we leave out?"

"Coupla things. First off it galls me somethin' fierce to leave you."

"Get past it, I have. Like Nacho's bunch sez 'Life is compromise.'"

"Also I sorta been wonderin' if, well…if you had any advice?"

The old man did not hesitate. Leaning forward, he said, "Keep it pure yet simple, respect yourself an' others, listen to your heart an' remember nothin's won if it ain't fun. An' if city folk seeya as a rube'n wanta test your willpower make it their problem…an stay away from that tequila." Calling it 'ta kill ya.'

"Yessir. Pure D Code of the West's always the best way to go." Then: "That's good advice, thank ya kindly."

Granpa grunted and said, "Awww, I'm fulla bull an' you know it." They were quiet until the old man said, "You're leavin' us tonight?"

"Yessir. I like the night. Just me an' the highway an' the moon'n stars."

"I'm gonna miss your pickin'n strummin' 'cause ya sure got a fine feelin' in your fingers. Makes for fine whittlin' inspiration for an old porch lizard like me."

Jack heard the bentwood rocker creak as his grandfather leaned back and started rocking slowly. It told Jack that something was happening down on the river and, sure enough, there was Nacho on the move, using a sotol stalk to guide his two burros to the water's edge.

"What all ya figure on learnin' down there in Austin, Ben Jack?"

"Hard to say other than I'd like to know why the Chisos are blue. Maybe I'll know by Christmas…be okay with you if I come home then?"

"That'd be fine'n dandy."

"You want anything from the Capital City?"

"Yep. Take that old Brownie box camera with ya'n get me a snapshot of the University of Texas Tower so's I can see where my tax dollars is goin'."

"Aw, Granpa, everybody knows you don't pay taxes." Then, sighting in on a boat exiting Santa Elena Canyon, Jack said, "Here come Los Boys."

"Yep, drifting wood," Granpa Gage said. The old man then groaned as he reached down to pick up the bottle of Senor Fuego and take a swig. "Here's to you young'uns. From whut I can figure from my readin'"—nodding at the magazines and newspapers—"a change in the weather is comin' this way."

"It's a little early for a norther, Granpa."

"Smart aleck kid!" Then: "But mebbe your bunch is what this country needs." After taking another swig from Senor Fuego, the old man winced and said, "Seems like when you get to be my age an' worn to a frazzle, life ain't so much a gift as a loan. Mebbe it's like Nacho says, we got more time than life."

There was a silence while Granpa hung his head and Jack again looked off at the Chisos. Finally, Jack said, "Would it be okay if I played your favorite song?"

"Yes, indeedy. Hearin' you play 'Waitin' for a Train' pleasures me dang near as much as seein' a passel of Big Bend Bluebonnets in springtime."

# CHAPTER TWO

*A visit from her only grandchild was special enough for Jen, but when Tres said he wanted her to tell him about the '60s Jack saw her come alive in a way he had not seen since the band took the stage that day at the Hill on the Moon Love-in. The first thing Jen did was to send Tres to a nearby cupboard and fetch a shoe box whose lid said "1968 Photos, 19th and University". When Jen set the shoe box in her lap and opened it, she said:*

*"I wouldn't trade this stuff for love nor money. The things inside this box are like holding time in your hands. They go back to before we started to shoot lightning through the sky. The slingshot stock on top was carved by Jack's Granpa and the photos were taken with my momma and daddy's camera."*

*"Was your mom pretty like you, Gram?"*

*Jen stayed silent as she looked at the letter from her father and his .38 Special. Then: "Well, it wasn't that my daddy was rich or that my momma was goodlookin'—though Momma was a beauty operator and that didn't hurt. Awww, piffle—I hope I don't bust out bawlin' like a baby."*

*"Just tell the story, Gram," Tres said. "Please tell it."*

· · ·

Jen had always said that Jack's very first words to her were "Yes, ma'am."

The first time Jack and Jen ever saw each other was the spring of 1965 at the Texas Theatre. She was in Austin for a Latin Club conference at the Commodore Perry Hotel and Jack had come for Boy's State. Jolinda Biggs had talked Jen into sneaking out to see *And God Created Woman* with Brigitte Bardot and, as fate would have it, Jack's cousin Michael A. had talked him into a getting a gander at the French sexpot, too. Even better, it turned out that the sneak preview was *Tom Jones* starring Albert Finny as a rube from the country finding his way in the world. Between movies Jen went to the lobby for a Mounds Bar. She got to the refreshment counter at the same time as a cute guy in Levis, white T-shirt and beat-up cowboy boots. Jen's first thought was Jack reminded her of James Dean in the movie *Giant*.

Jack showed right away that he was a gentleman by letting Jen go first.

The second time Jen saw Jack was months later, the Sunday morning before fall registration began at the University of Texas. Jen had left Fort Worth that morning in her high school graduation gift, a brand new orange Ford Mustang with white interior and automatic transmission. Jen called it 'the Pony.' In the Pony's trunk Jen's clothes were in her new set of olive green Samsonite luggage. On the back seat were her Gibson guitar and a case of Spraynet hairspray. On the passenger side bucket seat were Jen's purse and a new 35 mm Pentax camera—one of her father's two going away gifts, the other being a .38 Special he had put in the glove compartment for "just in case."

The drive south down Interstate 35 had been uneventful. For much of the drive Jen thought of her parents, how each was two people. She had a mom who, as far as the outside world was concerned, was June Cleaver of the *Leave It To Beaver* TV show. But there was another side to Jen's mom that in no way resembled June Cleaver. Likewise, Jen had a dad who in public acted like Robert Young's Jim Anderson on *Father Knows Best*. But he, too, had an entirely different side to him. In the driveway that morning her mom's parting advice for college had been "Now listen here, young lady, you've got personality as well as a cute figure, a perfect smile and sapphire eyes like Elizabeth Taylor—so don't give it away." Meanwhile, her father's advice had been his term for approval: "You're on, girl." Then: "You've got spunk but watch out for silver-tongued devils."

Jen arrived in Austin at a little before eight a.m. Because her father wanted photos of the Capitol Building and the University of Texas Tower, Jen exited I-35 at Sixth Street, and drove west the few blocks to Congress Avenue. Here she had to use caution before turning onto Congress because a shiny yellow old model pickup was gunning it to make the traffic light. Only later would she realize this was Jack, who had crossed Town Lake via the Congress Avenue Bridge and had noted that, though the lights were not synchronized, he could make it through them if he kicked the Fitty Six up to thirty-five miles an hour. Jack had driven past the Sheraton Crest Hotel to the east, Rosie's Tamale House to the west plus the Woolworth's and Scarborough's Department Store on his left when he almost ran a red light at Sixth Street. As a result, Jack slowed to twenty-five so as not to get a speeding ticket.

Meanwhile, Jen had turned right into Congress Avenue's northbound right lane and was going past Piccadilly Cafeteria on her right. The Capitol Building was dead ahead now as she drove past the angle parking on both sides of Congress Avenue. But Jen had to move the Pony over into the left lane to get past Jack poking along in the right lane. The next five blocks the Pony and the Fitty Six kept pace with one another because they were going from one red light to another. Human nature being what it is, Jack and Jen were soon looking over at each another.

The pickup and the Pony continued their parallel paths all the way to Twelfth Street, where Jack let Jen go straight ahead as Congress Avenue narrowed to the one lane that was Capitol Drive. When Jen pulled the Pony over in front of the Capitol Building, Jack did the same. Jen took her photo then drove around the Capitol Building to its north side where there was a view of the University of Texas Tower. She had pulled the Pony over at the end of Capitol Drive, where the north part of Congress Avenue began. When the Fitty Six again pulled up behind her and Jack got out, Jen said:

"Would you please take a photo of me in front of the Tower?"

"Yes, ma'am."

Jack had difficulty opening the Pentax's leather case, but Jen got her picture taken. Afterwards she asked if Jack was enrolled in the University.

"Yes, ma'am."

"Are you from Texas?"

"Yes, ma'am. I'm from down along the Rio Grande."

"It's a big river."

"Yes, ma'am."

"What I'm asking," Jen said, starting to grin, "is what town are from?"

"I'm not from a town. I'm off a ranch about a mile south of Terlingua."

Jen had never heard of Terlingua but she let it go when she saw Jack's Mexican six string in the cab of the Fitty Six, she said, "Do you play guitar?"

"Yes, ma'am."

Not mentioning that she played guitar, too, Jen said, "Is this your pickup?"

"Yes, ma'am. It's a 1956 Ford with a 292 cubic inch V-8 engine."

"And what's that?" Pointing at *Analuz* in the bed of the Fitty Six.

"It's a *cayuco*, ma'am, a mahogany log hollowed out into a canoe."

Now pointing at the canoe's name on the bow, Jen said, "Ann-uh–luhz?"

"Ah-nah-*loos*."

"Do you go down the Rio Grande in *Analuz*?"

"Yes, ma'am." Then Jack put his hand in his back pocket and said, "But not all the way." Next, grinning shyly, he said, "I hear it's a big river."

Smiling her perfect smile, Jen said, "Are you a silver-tongued devil?"

"Say whut?"

"Never mind." Then: "Have you ever been to Austin before?"

"Yes, ma'am." Also smiling. "I was here back in the spring."

"Didn't I see you at the Texas Theatre?"

"Yes, ma'am."

"I thought so. You were the cowboy at the candy counter."

"Yes, ma'am."

. . .

For years the the University of Texas included more than sixty buildings divided by Speedway, an inner campus drive. The University's eastern border was Interstate 35 and Guadalupe Street—"the Drag—was its western border. The north end of campus was 26th Street and from there the western half of campus ran south to 21st Street while the eastern half was two blocks longer and extended to 19th Street. But in 1965 post War World Two's population explosion of baby boomers began showing up and in three years University enrollment doubled. Traditional student housing being overwhelmed, a city of 190,000 now had a swollen center with 40,000 students, faculty and staff.

An anthill of social change.

A cultural crossroads of the 1960s.

# CHAPTER THREE

The next time Jack and Jen saw each other that fall of 1965 was outside Jen's dormitory, Helen M. Kirby Hall. It was the week after classes had begun and Jen was parked in the Pony on the corner of 29th Street and Whitis Avenue. She was listening to Radio KNOW's Jay Jackson spin the platters, Bob Dylan's "Like A Rolling Stone" now playing, part of KNOW's promotion of Dylan's upcoming concert at Palmer Auditorium. When the Fitty Six pulled up behind Jen, she saw Jack and another guy get out with a hand cart and quickly go up the sidewalk to enter a side door. Once again Jack wore Levis, white T-shirt and beat-up cowboy boots and his accomplice, a shorter guy with curly dark hair, had on madras Bermuda shorts, gray sweatshirt with the sleeves cut out and on his sockless feet were white canvass Converse sneakers. Soon Jack and his buddy exited the side door, the hand cart stacked high with cartons of empty soda bottles. At the Fitty Six the other guy lowered the tail gate to pull down a ramp for Jack to roll the hand cart into the pickup's bed. A moment later, the Fitty Six sped away, tires squealing past the Pony onto 29th Street.

Jen next saw Jack at the Dylan concert, but he did not see her. Once again he was with the curly-haired guy and they were up front in the VIP seats.

Jack and Jen did not see each other again until a year later, late in the evening of September 17, 1966. By now Jen was a 'Greek,' a member of Nu Mu Phi sorority and this was the weekend when the Nu Mus had game dates with the Gamma Sigma fraternity guys. The students around Jen at the game in Memorial Stadium on Red River between 21st and 23rd Streets were a meld of blue eyes and turned-up noses, almost all of them well-coiffed thanks to razor cut, blow-dried or permed hair. Their Clearasil skin reeked of Vitalis and Spraynet and English Leather and Old Spice toilet water and their breath of Lone Star and Schlitz beer or Cutty Sark and Chivas Regal that would later be covered up with Toddle House hash browns and Night Hawk steaks and omelets. Their teeth were orthodontist-perfectly-straight with cavities galore and their zits courtesy of Three Musketeers and Oreos and Betty Crocker. They were decked out in starched Levis and Clyde Campbell's Men Shop Arrow banlon shirts or cotton culottes and Scarborough Department Store skirts, cordovans and Burlington Gold Cup socks and penny loafers on their pink toe-ed feet.

Jen's date for the big game with the University of Southern California was a Gamma Sigma legacy from Houston, a 'legacy' which meant he had relatives who were Gamma Sigs. Jen's Gamma Sig legacy was a junior pre law major called "Kilroy" by Jen's sorority sisters because he was a groper when snockered on the bourbon in the flask in his burnt orange sweater. According to Jen's sister Nu Mu:

"Dating Kilroy is part of inter fraternity B.S. Ya got to go along to get along."

"Why is he called 'Kilroy'?"

"It's from World War II. 'Kilroy was here' was graffiti our boys left everywhere." Jolinda then began grabbing her body parts while saying "Kilroy was here...and here...here."

Forewarned being forearmed, on game night Jen wore culottes and under her white blouse a size 32B Maidenform bra. This particular Maidenform opened from the front via not one but two clasps and Jen figured it was hindrance enough to keep a snockered Kilroy off first base. Kilroy was so upset about the Horns 10-6 loss to Southern Cal that he wanted UT Coach Darrel Royal fired and USC's O.J. Simpson lynched for scoring the winning touchdown. Jen was ready to bolt, quit the scene when, north of 38th Street on Guadalupe, Kilroy pulled over his 1966 white Thunderbird to puke. Seeing Jack's Fitty Six parked in front of Hyde Park Recreation Club, Jen made her getaway. Inside the Club it was a testosterone pit, a smoke-filled pool hall teeming with the racket males made whenever they ensconced themselves in a competitive indoor environment. Jen's entry was like someone had yelled "Freeze, suckers!" because right away the racket subsided to eerily quiet. The patrons—University students, a few older redneck types—stopped shooting pool. Cue balls stopped being struck by cue sticks. Guys froze bent over with their butts in the air and stopped lining up pool shots. Mouths dropped open, cigarettes drooped and dangled from bottom lips. All eyes were on Jen. It was like she had walked through the wrong door into a men's locker room full of guys wearing nothing but their skivvies or jockey straps or towels around their waists or nothing at all, were bare ass buck naked after coming out of the shower. Jen felt like an alien who had just dropped in from outer space. But Jen did not say, "Take me to your leader." Not Jen. No, she stood her ground there in the silence and calmly scanned the pool hall while being ogled.

Meanwhile, Jack was nearby at a pair of pay phones. He was once again in his white T-shirt, Levis and beat-up cowboy boots, his thumbs tucked into the front pockets of his Levis, his left leg bent at the knee, his boot against the wall. Beside him was his buddy with curly dark hair, madras Bermuda shorts, gray sweatshirt with the sleeves cut out and white Converse sneakers with no socks. A stickpin on his chest said *Don't trust anyone over thirty.* Jen watched as the guy scammed the phone company: his left hand holding both receivers, one mouthpiece over the earpiece of the other while his right hand fed coins into the pay phone on his right. After the guy pushed the coin return and pocketed the coins he had just deposited, he saw Jen watching him, so he gave her a wink and said into the scammed phone:

"Hello? Saigon? That you, Saigon?"

This was when Jack saw Jen and came over to her. Also when an older guy in slacks and a faded sport shirt showed up. Clearly irritated, he pointed to a sign on the door saying NO WOMEN ALLOWED and said:

"Take it outside, honey. Hyde Park Recreation Club is men only."

So Jen took Jack by the arm and, going out the door, said, "We'll be back."

The manager said, "*He*"—pointing at Jack—"is welcome. *You* ain't."

"Oh, I don't mean him," Jen said. "I mean we *women* will be back."

Jen then showed the guy her perfect smile and left with her head held high.

. . .

After that, Jack and Jen were always on the lookout for each other. Their different worlds started to line up in J.M. Coetzee's sophomore English class in Room 301 of the English Building. Though Jen already knew Jack was bashful, in Room 301 she learned that he could be quite erudite when called upon by Mr. Coetzee, a South African who would go on to win the Nobel Prize for Literature. And Jen liked it when Jack began to grow his dark hair long and went from his beat-up cowboy boots to sockless moccasins. She found herself taken by Jack's quiet way. Unlike her father, who yelled a lot, Jack was a gentle soul with nary a yell in him. Also he was naturally cool. He could come off as "aww shucks" simple—which was kind of nice—but he could also come up with stuff like, "My pride and dignity are the integrity that holds my honor together. I believe we live a little each day or die a little each day…all by our own hand."

Jack was not a frat rat, so socially Jack and Jen did not run in the same circles. Being a Nu Mu was a full schedule outside of class and as Jen got further along at the University she found herself less and less stimulated by her sorority sisters' lifestyle. So much so that, by the end of her sophomore year, she was fed up with the Nu Mu ways.

It also impressed Jen to learn that Jack worked for a dollar an hour as a page at the main library. Jack and Jen started studying together there and, because Jack could get them into the stacks, the seventeen floors of books usually restricted to graduate students only, Jen entered a wider world. She met people not in Nu Mu world: folks with different ideas and goals an unusual perceptions. Folks seeking something besides a house in the suburbs with a pool and a maid.

Jack and Jen were not going steady and they were a million miles away from being lovers because Jack was too shy and Jen could not yet break away from her upbringing to make the first move. They were study buddies and pals, fast friends. They went to Nau's Drug for vanilla milk shakes. They looked for surprises in Cracker Jack boxes. It was Jack who got Jen to go to the Chuck Wagon, a social no-no for a Nu Mu. Also, they began playing music together. They talked of doing a duet at the Catholic student center or on the Student Union's patio. They played Ian and Sylvia songs but they acted like they were Dylan and Joan Baez. Jack told Jen his dream was to be in a rhythm and blues band and play in a downtown dive. Jen, trying to be spontaneous, said she just wanted to find her voice and that it sort of scared her how music was such a high.

It was not Jack, though, but an older student named Janis who nudged Jen forward in her music. Jack took Jen to Folk Sing, first door to the right when you went into the Student Union through the south entrance. There Janis took to Jen right away, proclaiming Jen to have a songbird voice but that it lacked body and soul. Though Janis had played at folk venues like The Id on 24th Street and Threadgill's on North Lamar, Janis saw herself as a blues singer. In the short time they knew each other Janis taught Jen "Trouble in Mind" and "I Know You Rider" and predicted that if Jen stopped trying to imitate Judy Collins and Joan Baez and listened to her heart, she would find her voice. According to Janis, this was like giving birth to a kid, like having a growth in your gut that one day would become the heart of the matter and show Jen who she really was. In May, 1966, as Janis was about to hitchhike to San Francisco with a guy named Travis, she took Jen to what Janis called "a place of transformation," a place where Jen could get away, find not only her voice but herself. Located behind Kirby Hall, this place of transformation was a limestone grotto under an oak tree on a bend

19

in Waller Creek. In time the oak became Jen's "wailing tree," a place to let it all out without witnesses while seated on a concrete bench that was a memorial to a daughter lost to polio in the 1950s.

Meanwhile, as kismet would have it, propinquity tightened Jack and Jen's bond because where Jack lived—Aunt Sofi's garage apartment—was a hundred yards away on Hemphill Park. So Jack and Jen started making music together in that limestone grotto on a bend of Waller Creek. Their first ever song together "I Know You Rider."

Then, right after Christmas break in January, 1966, after a wicked blue norther had whipped through Texas like a killer buzz saw, a blue Jack showed up in the grotto. Jen saw him pull up on Whitis Avenue in the Fitty Six, a Bentwood rocker and *Analuz* in the pickup's bed. He got out of the pickup and walked toward her with the saddest expression Jen had ever seen. He was without his Mexican guitar and was wearing Granpa Gage's Lucchese boots.

Jen was kidding when she said, "Why so blue, you? Who died?"

"A man I knew, someone I used to talk to. The norther finished him off."

· · ·

Jack and Jen stayed tight and they got through the death of Granpa Gage. But they very nearly did not get through what happened to Jen's parents a year later, a nightmare that began with a soft rapping on Jen's dorm room door.

At the end of the worst week in Jen's life, Christmas break, December, 1967, Jen was alone in the limestone grotto. For the first time she had not brought her Gibson guitar, just her purse. Jolinda Biggs had just driven Jen back from Greenwood Cemetery off White Settlement Road in Fort Worth where they had attended her parents' double funeral. Two people who had stopped loving one another would now lie beside each other for eternity. The first real clue to her parents' downfall had come right before Christmas when her 1965 orange Ford Mustang—her Pony—was repossessed. A phoned call home got no answer.

20

Next came the insistent rapping at her door that changed her life forever.

It took a while for Jen to grasp what had happened. She guessed her mom could not stand success and her father could not face failure. Her mom had told her during their last phone call that she wanted a divorce but Jen would not believe it. She now realized she should have seen it coming when her mom had given up the Metrical for Lunch Bunch in favor of mother's little helpers and vodka—booze Jen's dad could not smell, but he sure could see it. Their fights over the last year had only seemed to make her mom drink more and her father smoke more. In public they had faked it.

It had not really bothered Jen that she would soon no longer be a Nu Mu. But, besides her clothes, all she had in the world was her mom's heirloom hair brush, her Smith Corona portable typewriter, her Samsonite luggage, her Gibson guitar, the yogurt maker from Neiman Marcus she was going to give her parents for Christmas—and the "Just in case" .38 Special in her purse that now took on a new meaning for Jen as in "Just in case the world ended"… which it had. For Jen there were no tears, just a sullen despair that only Jack could coax her out of. There in the grotto Jen had on a face that she had never shown before, a face that had shown up in the mirror at the outset of puberty. Her parents had never seen it; no one had. It was a solemn face, one bereft of hope and full of an almost stoic despondency. An adult face. Jen was deep into this face, telling herself, "I won't cry, no, I won't shed a tear." But a lone tear did appear in one eye as she closed her eyes one final time, her hand on the .38 Special in her purse. She had just started humming "I Know You Rider" when she heard Jack's voice say:

"I read in the paper where you've been orphaned too."

Jen's eyes opened and the face she would not show went away, taking the lone tear with it. "Oh, wow," she said, "I didn't know it was in the Austin paper."

"What're you gonna do?"

"I haven't the faintest idea. I have no place to live. I have no plan. I'm not trained for anything but being a student. I'm broke and my parents left debts I have to pay—something I know nothing about because I was always on the receiving end of the Lay-A-Way or Installment Plan."

Jack said, "Yep, the future's pretty bleak for us two orphans." Then: "Want to go down to the water an' take a spin in *Analuz*? There's a place I've never been before that I'd like to see."

· · ·

They were in *Analuz*. There was an early morning rain and the night's waning moonlight was shining on Lake Austin. Jen was leaning backwards on Jack's chest and his chin was resting atop her head when he took hold of her shoulders to get her full attention as he leaned forward to whisper in her right ear:

"Jennifer, you and I are in the wind now. We're adrift with almost no one to trust or rely upon."

"I got nobody. Absolutely nobody."

"You got me and I got family so we're not in the grip of desperation yet. My Grandfather Nacho's a strong and centered person who's in a place right now that my other granpa said is an ancient crossroads that'd do me some justice. Goshdawg-it, I think I need that now—how 'bout you? Wanta go to Old Mexico'n see Nacho?"

"Sure. Why not?"

"I want so much to shield you from the pain and suffering, Jen."

"And I want the same for you, Jack."

# CHAPTER FOUR

*Tres said, "Palenque? Way back then, Gram?"*
  *"You've been there, yes?"*
  *"You know I have—you paid for it."*
  *"And was it worth it?"*
  *"Every penny."*

· · ·

It was winter solstice. Nacho said they were in "legendary time" and Jack and Jen felt sure he was right for never had they been anywhere so ancient yet vibrant.

It was nightfall in Palenque, a heaven-inspired ancient Maya city dominated by what la maya called sacred living mountains: five archaeological wonders built of limestone set on a hillside against a verdant cusp of Southwest Mexico's forested Chiapas Mountains. At sunset Nacho had led Jack and Jen into the residential structure named The Palace then up its three-story square tower to behold the sun's fall into the Underworld. From this outlook they could view the adjacent structure—the stacked pyramid-temple named The Temple of Inscriptions—just as Father Sun's daily journey to death pierced the temple atop the stacked pyramid with sunshine. According to Nacho, the sun "entered" the temple via the stairway in its floor that descended into God-King Hanab Pacal's tomb under the pyramid-temple. Scholars called this a hierophany but Nacho the daykeeper called it "a calamity of events featuring The Forces That Are."

Afterward, Nacho led Jack and Jen to the base of the Temple of Inscriptions and from there they went up to the pyramid-temple's summit via steep stone steps that led them past a pair of stone balustrades carved into kneeling figures whose faces were turned as if looking at whomever was ascending the stairs. Up in the temple, in the narrow gallery there, Nacho kindled branches from the sacred copal tree into a fire on the stone floor. Next Nacho took from his colorfully woven Maya rucksack their evening meal, their three faces flickering in the violets, reds, oranges and yellows of the coals in the fire as he prepared handmade tortillas of white corn with black beans and cilantro, onion and chiles and tomatoes, food with more flavor than Jen had ever known.

Once they had finished their meal and the stars above had become innumerable points of light set in a mantle of exquisite darkness, Nacho placed a red handwoven blanket beside the fire then a smoking brazier of copal incense on the top step of the stairway leading down to the royal tomb. Next he set out tomorrow morning's breakfast of golden mangoes, mamey, papaya, guanabana and finger-sized bananas and bid the lovers adieu saying "Someone's eyes must always greet the dawn." Then down the Temple of Inscription's steps he went playing a lilting serenade on his wooden flute.

Later that longest night of the year, on the outskirts of the temple, beside the top of that royal tomb's stairway, Jack took Nacho's gift to the lovers of a matrimonial hammock and strung its vibrant-as-a-rainbow strings between two of the temple's four enormous inner limestone columns, each dedicated on May 25, 690, each with a larger-than-life figure of Maya royalty holding a child.

And in that hammock Jack and Jen lay the longest of nights nestled in each other's arms. Jen did not sleep a wink. Not because she was on the lookout for bugs or other creepycrawlies. Nor was her sleeplessness from the lightning and thunder from nearby squalls or the maniacal screams of howler monkeys or even the mighty roar of la maya's ruler of the night, the jaguar, Maya icon for the sun after its fall into the Underworld. Jen lay awake partly due to the parade of stars overhead with names like Jaguar Eyes, The River of Time and Heart of Heaven. But mostly, Jen did not sleep because Palenque was a magical place in which she felt transformed.

24

As someone who had never been outside the United States, Mexico was more than just another country. It was a whole other world, a liberating experience whose feeling she did not want to relinquish after the recent tragic events and changes in her life. Now Jen was high on life, whereas a few days ago she had been down so low that she had been contemplating suicide.

For more than two days she and Jack had journeyed here in the Fitty Six, driving to The Vanilla Fudge's "The Beat Goes On" album and Cream's "Disraeli Gears" on an eight track car stereo Jack's cousin had loaned him. Jack drove and Jen looked out the window. Once in Palenque Jack and Jen partook of ancient rites of welcome conducted by Nacho, not only eating and laughing and dancing in ways they had never dreamed of but becoming enamored of la maya, the northern hemisphere's oldest living culture. A people who felt they knew where the center of the earth was and observed a way of life that articulated a gentle spirit of power and beauty that belied a divine wisdom. It was as if Jack and Jen had crash-landed into a piece of heaven, a rapture wherein they felt the presence of Jack's Granpa and Jen's parents—the good ones, June Cleaver and Jim Anderson—and that these three new spirits were with and within the new lovers yet not haunting them. They had simply crossed over to another side, become what Nacho called "breath upon the mirror."

"I feel as though I've been here before," Jen had said to Nacho.

"We Maya have always been here before," Nacho had replied. "And you are as much Maya as I for you are another like myself, for we are all Maya and what was old is new again." He had then placed a fist over his heart and said, "One world, one planet." As he tapped his heart with that fist, he said, "Forever here. Here forever."

"Good God," Jen had said, meaning it.

And Jack was as calm and serene as Jen had ever seen him while continually giving her that same certain smile she had been giving him. And when Jen lay back against his chest and said, "My biology professor Dr. Spear said that in nature it's the female who calls the first shot in mating … do you agree?" Jack's answer was:

"Yes, ma'am."

25

. . .

Jen's eyes were greeting the dawn. Which was an amazing transformation itself as Jen had never slept outside before: too many bugs.

At first light, as night's shadow diminished in substance, overtaken by dawn's twilight's transcendence into day, Jen was nestled like a cuddly cub into the hollow of Jack's shoulder. Unsure if she was dreaming, she peeked out from behind their red blanket to peer over the multi-hued strings of the hammock they shared like a nest. Her eyes widened, not from the crimson red dawn but with utter wonder, astounded as her gaze revolved slowly north then east at the Temple of Inscription's four companion "sacred living mountains" known as The Palace and the three smaller reverential temples to the east that archaeologists called The Group of the Cross. All around Jen the sky seemed at eye level, as if she and Jack were on the first of the thirteen levels of Maya heaven. In the meantime, dawn itself was being spawned behind a squall bawling amid streaks and glares of white sheet lightning dancing on the horizon. As, like Jen, Father Sun was reborn, Jen's head was filled with declarations like "eerie enchantment", "heavenly" and "singularly powerful." Palenque was indeed out of this world yet somehow also the center of this Island Earth.

Jen was now taking in this metaphysical sustenance as Lord Morningstar– Venus– smiled down upon her, blessed her through dawn's yellow-red tinged clouds. The moon that Nacho said was the closest to earth it had been in twenty years was beaming down a smile, too. Below, in the valley known as Toktan–"cloud center"–the wind now whipped up and over Rio Otolum's aqueduct through the ruins. As Nacho's wooden flute could be heard saluting this new day Jack stirred to kiss Jen on the neck and say:

"Someone's eyes must always greet the dawn."

"We're in heaven," Jen said. "I'm all better now. I'm new, I'm one again…maybe for the first time."

Jack said. "We are two new lovers holding hands at the end of a rainbow."

"And our love is its pot of gold." Then, giggling: "It is bigger than both of us, isn't it?"

Holding her closer, Jack said, "Maybe we can share in something rare."

"You're on," Jen said.

What they did share that dreamlike dawn, there in their matrimonial hammock above the stone floor of a sacred living mountain, was a reverie within the coals, flames and smoke of their campfire atop the Temple of Inscriptions. Jen's arms twined around Jack's neck and she grinned in delirium as she used the knuckle of her right index finger to caress his right ear—something she had seen Ingrid Bergman do to Cary Grant in *Notorious*. In the coals she believed they were seeing into the future, viewing a fine and private place in time where they lay together beneath their blanket while communicating via what la maya called the "Language of Touch." Jen was feeling eternally wild with a power, her body tight against Jack's and exuding a long, low moan as she patted his hand and said:

"Your feet are cold."

"But my lips are warm," he said then kissed her.

"Warm is not the word—they're on fire."

# CHAPTER FIVE

They came down from heaven and went back up to Texas. Now they were a couple, nothing between them in the cab of the Fitty Six but the slight space between their slender waists. On the drive to Austin they made a pact:

"We are three: you, me and us. We fight for you, we fight for me, we fight for *us*. We don't live *for* each other, we live *within* each other.

It was mid morning, Wednesday, January 3, 1968. All their possessions were in the Fitty Six. Jack had little money, only a part-time minimum wage job at the main library. Jen had even less than Jack, so it had been decided that Jen would also get a job at the main library and that both would toil at whatever else could help cover their living and tuition costs. When Jack suggested making a buck or two playing for spare change down on the Drag, Jen wondered aloud if that would be begging. Jack said, "No, we won't be beggars, we'll be troubadours." Jen then said, "Yeah—*wander*ing troubadours 'cause we don't even have a place to sleep tonight." When Jack said they would sleep in the bed of the truck if they had to, Jen said, "But all our stuff's in our 'bed' and there's a norther." Jack said they would stay with his cousin, a man of ways and means.

The temperature was forty degrees when Jack parked the Fitty Six on 21st Street across from Littlefield Fountain. Walking north up the South Mall, Jack told Jen that this time of day Cousin Michael A. usually could be found in the Student Union's Chuck Wagon. Since it was between semesters, few folks were out. Only a smattering of students and staff were ambling up and down the mall or in and out of the academic buildings that lined it: the Music Building then the English Building to Jack and Jen's left and, on their right, Benedict Hall, Mezes Hall and Batts Hall. Jack and Jen both wore jeans and jean jackets, Jack in a long-sleeved white guayabera shirt, Jen in a Mexican wedding shirt, both shirts and the colorfully woven Maya rucksack each carried were gifts from Nacho. Jack again had on Granpa Gage's Lucchesse boots while Jen flip-flopped along in two more gifts from Nacho: Maya sandals and red wool socks. After making a left at Battle Hall onto the west mall they ascended the Student Union's steps. Here Jack took a *Daily Texan* from its dispenser, its headline reading:

*Half a million Americans in Vietnam*

"Rats," Jen said.

. . .

The Chuck Wagon was a student cafeteria through whose double glass doors Fontella Bass was singing "Rescue Me" on the juke box. As Jack led Jen toward the west wall past orange vinyl chairs around tables with white Formica tabletops, he told her that Michael A. liked to call himself a "Mexamerileb" because he was Mexican-American and Lebanese. Jack said the Chuck Wagon was Michael A.'s office, where he scalped tickets to UT sporting events and concerts at Palmer Municipal Auditorium. When Jack said that Michael A. was the guy in the Hyde Park Recreation Club back in '66, Jen frowned and said:

"The guy scamming long distance phone calls was your *cousin*?"

"Yep. Michael A. claims to have a commercial mind but he's really just trying to get a leg up on life. He's not as laid back as me 'cause he's into dynamic tension. And don't freak out when he calls you 'darlin'—he's just bein' impish on account of he's such a stinker."

"Anything else?"

"He's a darn good singer."

When Michael A. saw Jack and Jen approaching, he lowered his rose colored glasses to give Jen the onceover then gave Jack a nod of approval. Michael A.'s dark curly hair was longer than when Jen had seen him in the Hyde Park Recreation Club back in 1966, but he again had on faded Levis, a tattered gray sweat shirt and white

30

low cut Converse sneakers without socks. Thrown over the back of his chair was an officer's Navy pea coat, the kind with leather on the pockets and collar. On the pea coat's lapel Jen saw a button saying *Reality is a crutch* and in the open briefcase in front of Michael A. were *Catch 22, One Flew Over the Cuckoo's Nest, The Art of Loving* and *The Kama Sutra.* Seated beside Michael A. was a guy in a wool sweater, khaki pants and desert boots who gave Jack a nod then stood up and left. As Michael A. called after him, "Hey, play E-3 on the juke," Jen saw a white vinyl clipboard hooked to one of the guy's belt loops beside a leather slide rule scabbard with **TAJ** neatly written on it. When Jack introduced Jen as "my girl Jen" Michael A. said:

"*Welll!* Two and a half years of college and my cowboy cousin finally lands one! Splendid, Cuz! *Splendid!* The slumming debutante and the cosmic yahoo of the Rio Bravo, eh?" Then he winked at Jen and said, "Gotta a kiss for us kinfolk?"

Showing her perfect smile, Jen said, "Now, now, we're not kissing kin yet."

"All in good time, darlin', all in good time." Then: "So what's your story, morning glory? Do you scold? Nag?" Still getting only the perfect smile, he said, "You a Tri Delt? Chi Omega? Pi Phi?"

"I was a Nu Mu but now I'm inactive."

"Welcome to the counter-culture," Michael A. said. "I happen to know a little about tuning in, turning on and dropping out myself. Where're you from?"

"Fort Worth."

"Ahhh, Fort Worth. Where the West Begins. Harold Maples' political cartoons in the *Star Telegram*, Mrs. Baird's Bread, Van Cliburn, oil and gas moguls, country clubs." Raising his eyebrows, he said, "Rivercrest? Shady Oaks? Colonial?"

"Colonial Country Club," Jen said. "Also inactive."

"What's your daddy do?"

"Jen's just been orphaned," Jack said. "It happened right before Christmas."

"Heavy," Michael A. said, wincing. "A nasty calamity of events but *caca pasa, chachalaca* and at least you two orphans got each other an' nobody starves in America—yet. Of course, nobody rides for free either."

Jack said, "Jen's new to the system."

"I'm hip. End of sheltered upbringing, must now learn The Fine art of Hanging Out in the 60's—actually, I'm half orphaned myself."

"His daddy's in the army," Jack said to Jen. "He's a captain in Vietnam."

"Another stupid human mistake, the Vietnam War," Michael A. said. "Now tell me about your visit to that land time ain't forgot."

"Mexico was cool," Jack said, "and Palenque's a place of the gods."

"I believe it, every word," Michael A. said. "And how is our grandfather?"

"Nacho's the same as ever only more so," Jack said. "He's still a force."

"There ain't another like him or Granpa Gage," Michael A. said.

Next, as E-3 came on the juke box—Cream's live version of Robert Johnson's "Crossroads"—Michael A. and Jen saw Jack come alive: bobbing his head, tapping his Luccheses to the beat, even fingering Eric Clapton's guitar lead. Still moving to the juke box music, Jack said:

"Who is this Taj guy anyway?"

"Taj? Oh, he's the same as you'n me in that he just wants to get an education, end racism and the war. He's also an electrical engineering phee-nom with so many cultural ties you can't label him. A real renaissance man is Taj."

"How do you know him?" Jack said.

"Uncle Tunoose introduced us. He said 'Taj is a great guy to have liking you'…which I hope is true since Taj'n me is gonna be sharing digs."

Now no longer moving to the music, Jack said, "*Newww* digs?"

"Yep. Me'n Thelma an' Barney Lou'n Taj got us a house."

"'Coool," Jack said, "because me'n Jen need a place to crash."

"I dunno," Jen said to Jack. "Six people in a house is an awful lot."

"Thelma'n Barney Lou are goldfish not people," Jack said.

32

Her perfect smile back on, Jen said, "We are kind of in a bind… Cuz."

"I'm hip, seein' as how registration's next week," Michael A. said. "Actually you two showing up is providential."

"Oh? How so?" Jen said, trying not to furrow her brow.

"Why crash at my place when we can share a pad?"

"Like I said," Jack said to Jen, "Cuz is a man of ways an' means."

"How big is this 'pad'?" said Jen.

"Actually, it' a house" A big 'un. Two stories, five bedrooms, three up, two down, three baths, living room, dining room. It's got oak floors, high ceilings, tall windows an' has turn of the century charm, history an' rustic ambiance. It was built in 1905 an' was very swanky in its day—an eminently casual pad for y'all two to play house in."

"How close to campus is it?" Jen said.

"Two blocks"–pointing south–"corner of 19th and University. *Splendid* location. I parked my motorcycle there today."

Jen said, "Does this old house need anything?"

"Just we three an' Taj, maybe one more for the fifth bedroom. We'll need some furniture'n kitchen appliances. The place was previously the Waterloo Music Academy. Nobody's lived there for twenty years."

"Who's the lessor?"

"Uncle Tunoose."

"Whoa!" Jack said. "Is that old pool parlor dude into real estate now?"

"Check. 'Buy land', he says, 'they ain't making any more.' See, what happened is, after the Waterloo Music Academy went under, Uncle Tunoose waited until he could get it cheap. His plan is for the University to buy it since, thanks to us baby boomers, UT is gonna need more land."

"So you're saying we can get kicked out at any time?" Jen said.

"Nothin' lasts forever, darlin.' Stuff happens. *Caca pasa, chachalaca.*"

"What would our rent be?" Jack asked.

"Ahhh, yes," Michael A. said. "The rent situation, baksheesh."

"For our own bedroom and bathroom," Jen said.

33

"Let's see now, for two lovers? One's a cousin so we're talking family rate." Michael A. now pretended to do some figuring before saying, "Ohhh, sayyy twenty a month?" Spreading his arms in a benign gesture, he said, "How's that grab ya?"

"That's not bad, Jen," Jack said. "We can afford that."

Jen said, "How much is the deposit?"

"Zero, zip, nada."

"And the utility bills?" Jen said. "How much will they cost us?"

"Zilch."

"How come?"

"Goshdawg-it, Jen," Jack said, "don't look a gift horse in the mouth."

Frowning, Jen said, "Does it have electricity?"

"Yesss, but some wiring's in need of repair. But Taj is on it, he'll handle it."

Jen said, "You're sure this place is livable?"

"You durn betcha. I'm moving in today." Then, grinning: "Wanta hear the good part?"

Jen said, "What about running water? We gotta have running water."

"Not a problem. What are you anyway? Pre-law? An accounting major?"

"English major minoring in psychology. And in this dog-eat-dog world I happen to be very vulnerable right now and my father warned me about guys like you." Then Jen leaned over to whisper in Jack's ear, "Your cousin's a silver-tongued devil if there ever was one."

"But the rent's affordable," he whispered back "and life is compromise."

Jen let out an uncomfortable sigh and said to Michael A., "Communal living? We split the food, cooking and cleaning?"

"We can give it a shot," he said.

Jen was thoughtful now, her brow furrowed, her fingers drumming the white Formica tabletop. "Just where would *your* bedroom be?"

"I'm taking the whole downstairs."

34

"That's negotiable," Jen said. Then, to Jack: "Okay. We earn a dollar an hour at the library, twenty hours a week. That's $80 each a month, $160 altogether."

Jack said, "We don't get the whole one-sixty."

Jen's brow furrowed more than ever. "How come?"

"The government takes its cut," Michael A. said. "Social Security, withholding, all like that." Leaning forward, he said, "Everybody wants a piece of you out here in the cold, cruel world, darlin'."

"I believe it, every word," Jen said, giving Michael A. a knowing look.

Next, drumming her fingers some more, brow furrowed she let out a long sigh and said, "Does this place have shade trees?"

"Yesss," Michael A. said, sounding tired. "What say we go see the house so it can answer your questions instead of me?"

Right away Jen stood up and said, "You're onnn."

# CHAPTER SIX

They left the Chuck Wagon, went down the hallway and were exiting via the south door when a woman hissed "*Jerk!*" at Michael A.

"That was Lenore," Jack whispered to Jen, "a disgruntled old flame."

They walked east on the West Mall, Michael A.'s curly dark hair and rose colored glasses down in his pea coat like a wary turtle in his shell. At the UT Tower they turned south, the Tower's main entrance behind them, etched in stone above it the University's motto:

"Ye Shall Know the Truth and the Truth Shall Set You Free."

Here another woman hissed at Michael A., saying: "*Pig!*"

"That was Daphne, another old flame," Jack whispered to Jen.

Now they were going down the South Mall, the long sweep of lawn where from his perch atop the UT Tower sniper Charles Whitman murdered students on August 1, 1966. After passing the English and Music Buildings, at Littlefield Fountain, about to cross 21st Street onto University Avenue, Michael A.'s rose colored glasses peered over the officer's pea coat and he said:

"Hey, there's the Fitty Six, so let's ride."

"It's only two blocks," Jen said.

Michael A. said, "Why walk when we can ride?"

"Because," Jen said, "the Fitty Six is a Ford pickup with a 292 cubic inch eight cylinder engine and gasoline is twenty-five cents a gallon."

"We're in a norther," Michael A. said. "I might catch my death."

"The norther's at our backs," Jen said.

Michael A. said, "I'll give ya a quarter for the fossil fuel—let's ride."

Jen, putting some whine in it, said, "Jaaack?"

Jack sighed and said, "The Fitty Six's in a primo parking spot, Cuz."

After a look of pure pity for his cousin, Michael A. walked.

. . .

Two blocks south on University Avenue's they came to the rear of a two-story red brick house where Michael A.'s burgundy Triumph 650 was in a wood-shingled garage beside a stoop leading to the house's back door. As Michael A. led them past five oaks on the sidewalk, Jack said to Jen:

"Shade trees, Jen."

They rounded the corner and went west to a concrete walkway with "200 W. 19th stenciled on it. This walkway led to the front steps and another walkway to a lower floor. Going up the front steps' dozen oak planks to a porch taking up half of 200 W. 19th's front, they halted before a screen door, the upper half of the front door behind it all glass. Here Michael A. stopped and said:

"This is a pretty cool pad for us counter-culture types."

"Sure is," Jack said.

"It needs paint," Jen said.

"Paint is overrated," Michael A. said then opened the screen door and yelled, "Hello in the house!" Getting no answer, he said, "Street people squat in vacant houses an' some are Vietnam vets so we best not barge in on 'em." Next he pulled the front door's old-timey ringer—only to have it break off in his hand.

"Bad omen," Jen said.

Jack said nothing, just pushed the front door open.

Inside was an eight-foot-wide entryway, oak flooring, high ceilings and walls with peeling plaster. To the right was a bedroom with a bathroom and directly in front of them was a second bedroom connected via a shared bathroom to a third bedroom. Left of the second bedroom a stairway went downstairs. Left of it was a living room half separated from the dining room by an 8' wide book case that went all the way to the ceiling. Beyond the dining room was the kitchen.

"It's clean," Michael A. said after removing his rose colored glasses.

"The light fixtures don't have covers or bulbs," Jen said.

"They were probably liberated by the street people," Michael A said. "But light bulbs're cheap'n 'Life beneath a bare light bulb' is high chic for us hippies."

Pointing at the first bedroom, Jen said, "There are no curtains in there."

"So use the curtains in one of the bedroom downstairs," said Michael A.

"The bathrooms have tubs but no shower heads," Jen said.

"All in due time," said Michael A. then gave Jack another look of pure pity.

"I don't see very many electrical outlets," Jen said.

"Even as we speak Taj is at the Engineering Lab liberating the electrical goodies needed for our new abode," said Michael A.

Frowning at this, Jen said, "Does 'liberating' mean 'stealing'?"

"Certainly not. To liberate is to redistribute the wealth," said Michael A.

"It'll all work out, Jen," Jack said. "Get behind this, willya?"

She sighed and said, "Well, I do like the high ceilings and oak trees."

"All in all an ideal pad," Michael A. said. "And I plan to make the downstairs conducive to petting and intercourse 'cause"—winking at Jen—"what goes around comes around."

"What's that supposed to mean?"

"That's the *goood* part I mentioned in the Chuck Wagon, Jen." Showing her his teeth as he said, "See, legend has it that this house was once a brothel."

"Nawww," Jack said. "A for-real house of ill repute?"

"Oh god," Jen said. "You're making the downstairs into a den of iniquity?"

"Now there's an idea," Michael A. said, eyebrows raised in mock surprise.

"You wouldn't dare," Jen said.

"Yeah, I would."

"Yeah," Jack said, "he would."

"But I won't. However, with a rustic ambiance and eminently casual—" Michael A. stopped talking because a creaking sound had come from downstairs.

"We are not alone," Jen said. "There's somebody else here."

Voice raised, Jack said, "Anybody there?"

No reply.

Frowning again, Jen said, "Do you think it's a street person?"

"Maybe it's Taj," Michael A. said. "Taj? Wherefore fart thou?" Getting no reply, he said, "It's the wind or a street person or …"

"Or what?" Jen said.

"Well, besides being a brothel there's more to this house's history. Our new pad may have a certain aesthetic essence that is"—lowering his voice to a whisper—"mayhaps a, uh, ghost named Mona."

"Cool," an elated Jack said. "Too, tooo *coool*."

"*Phooey!*" Jen said. Then: "And as for Jack and I moving in, Cuz, you're on."

"An' we got dibs on the front bedroom," Jack said to Michael A. Then, with his own look of pure pity: "And the downstairs is all yours, Cuz."

# CHAPTER SEVEN

Jack was saying, "To tell you the truth is, I've never bought furniture."

"Me either," Jen said. "I was spoiled and pampered and never had to buy any necessities with my own money."

"Not to worry," Michael A. said, "Today y'all two learn from a master."

It was getting near noon. First, they made room for their purchases. Jack took Granpa Gage's bentwood rocker out of the bed of the Fitty Six and set it on the front porch. Jen lugged her Samsonite luggage up to the front bedroom with Michael A. right behind toting Jack's duffle bag. Jack and Michael A. then took *Analuz* to the west side of the house. Next they all got in the Fitty Six and drove the half a dozen blocks to Oat Willie's on San Antonio Street at 18th Street where they took up Oat Willie's offer of two king-sized water beds, one for $19.99, another for a penny more. At Twelfth and Lamar, across from The Tavern, they had the Fitty Six filled up with ethyl. Michael A. chatted up the attendant while the guy checked the tires, oil and water. When the pump stopped at $4 even he got back into the Fitty Six.

"But we have to pay," Jen said.

Jack said, "We did pay—Cuz traded the guy two tickets to the Lavender Hill Express concert."

"Why buy when you can trade?" Michael A. said

Next they drove a couple of miles north on North Lamar, made a left at 2Js Hamburgers, went two blocks west then turned right onto Burnet Road. They went north some more until they passed 45th Street. Here they turned left into Big John's House of Crap. Once Michael A. and Big John had exchanged hugs and hushed words, Michael A. explained that Uncle Tunoose was the real owner of Big John's and thus they would be getting the family rate. So, for $5 they bought three shower heads, a faded red couch, $2 worth of fruit crates to be used as hippie-style clothes dressers and, for a buck a piece, two purple butterfly chairs and five scratched-up straight back chairs. In exchange for tickets to the Lavender Hill Express concert Big John threw in pots and pans for their kitchen needs. Michael A. got a black light, a lava lamp and a Judy Jetson lunch box with thermos. Jen bought a $10 Stromberg Carlson console television set because:

"We need the straight poop from Uncle Walter on the CBS Evening Blues."

"And *The Road Runner Show*," Jack said.

"And *Dark Shadows*," said Michael A.

Next, because Jack was starving, they stopped at Kirschner's Café further north on Burnet Road and had the 85-cent blue plate special: breaded veal cutlets covered in yellow cream gravy, fries, wedges of iceberg lettuce with sliced tomatoes and french dressing, iced tea plus a Black Cow milkshake for Michael A. By one o'clock they were at Ramon's Fine Imports on Airport Boulevard—another Uncle Tunoose enterprise—where they bought $3 worth of rice paper globes for the bare light bulbs and Indian prints for window curtains.

Further north on Airport Boulevard Jack went into Mrs. Johnson's Bakery and bought a dozen glazed donuts for 60 cents despite Jen chiding him that after midnight they would be half price at the drive-up window.

· · ·

The Fitty Six turned south off Comal Street in East Austin. Down an alley lined with the rear entrances of warehouses and junk shops, they found a man named Cool Breeze, a no-age black guy with a cheesy fedora, a pencil thin moustache and a toothpick in the corner of his mouth. For effect he spoke jive-ass-hipster. For clothes he wore baggy brown trousers, a red flowery long-sleeve shirt and high top black Converse sneakers. According to Michael A., whom Cool

Breeze called "Mister Hoochie Coochie Man," his real name was Jackson Lamar Brown. He was a guy who just looked guilty, on the run as he made sure nobody was watching before opening the trunk of a pink 1956 Cadillac. Inside were cases of Wild Turkey, Bacardi and new record albums. For $3 Jack got the new Cream album.

While Jack went inside Dead Meat Barbeque for chopped beef sandwiches, Cool Breeze showed his "newsed appliances" he kept under a tarp on a flatbed trailer. Jen, and Michael A. then selected a Hotpoint refrigerator with a clunky handle, a Tappan electric range with but two working burners, a new Waring blender and Sunbeam toaster. Next a Kenworth truck entered into the alley wheezing diesel fumes, Mexican license plates barely hanging on, its flatbed trailer stacked with "newsed refrigerators." Even before the driver got out of the Kenworth, Jen was frowning with concern and once the driver had unhooked the trailer and stepped over to Cool Breeze, palm held out for payment, Jen frowned some more. As Cool Breeze paid off the driver from a roll of bills that had been tucked in his cheesy fedora, Jen sidled up to Michael A. and, whispering, said:

"We're not by any chance buying stolen goods, are we?"

"Certainly not." Acting offended. "We're merely engaging in another form of the redistribution of wealth called 'recycling'."

"Yeah, right," Jen said to herself.

When the Kenworth driver left, Cool Breeze opened one of the "newsed" freezers to reveal brick-shaped packages wrapped in butcher paper. Jen, again whispering in Michael A.'s ear, said:

"What's he doing?"

"Inventory. Making sure Uncle Tunoose didn't get shorted."

"So,"—her brow furrowed, eyes closed in disbelief—"the packages are?..."

"Choice quality one-pound bricks. Nacho's stuff is the best."

It was an astonished Jen who said, "Nacho's in on this?"

Michael A. rolled his eyes and said, "Nacho is Mr. Big, darlin'."

"In Texas one itty bitty joint can get you ninety-nine years in prison."

Michael A. shrugged and said, "No risks, no riches."

Jen then said to the returning Jack, his mouth full of chopped beef sandwich: "We gotta go now."

"Sure thing, hon," Jack said and offered her a bite.

"Now, Jack, *nowww*," Jen said and began dragging Jack toward the Fitty Six.

But they had to wait until Michael A. and Cool Breeze loaded a large black door into the Fitty Six's bed. Once out of the alley and on Comal Street, Jen said:

"What in the world is that?" Meaning the large black door.

"A large black door," Michael A. said. "It came off a church."

Jen said, "It's a *church* door?"

"Sure thing." Nodding. "Pretty cool too, don't you think?"

"Why in the world a *church* door?"

"'Cause it appeals to me."

"Where did it come from? Was it stolen?"

"Now see here, darlin.' I'm not in charge of pedigree'n provenance for everything we lay our hands on. If the price is right, I don't quibble. So cool the paranoia bit an' just be glad you know me 'cause we got us some cut rate deals today." Then he gave Jack another look of pity while Jen gave Jack her own look.

"Come on, ya'll," Jack said, "when you get right down to it, it's all relative."

# CHAPTER EIGHT

Back at the house they found Taj wiring electrical outlets in Jack and Jen's bedroom. Jen thanked him then introduced herself—only to have an awkward moment because Taj did not say a word, just smiled and nodded. Michael A. then came up to put his arm around Taj's shoulders and say:

"Did I not mention that Taj is a mute?"

"Nooo, you most certainly did *not* mention that," Jen said smiling through her embarrassment.

"Good bloodlines too," Michael A. said. "A true man of the world. Bit of a diplomatic hodgepodge actually—dash of royalty here, some revolutionary there. His mother's Russian, father Chinese, has one French grandfather, one English, one grandmother Brazilian, one Swedish and I believe there's some gypsy blood too—man knows a ton of languages."

"So Taj is not only a pleasant presence he's Everyman." Jen said.

Jen then declined Michael's A.'s invitation to a "Wesson Oil Party" even though he acted hurt and said he merely wanted to commemorate moving into their new pad by pouring cooking oil on the kitchen floor and rolling down bare ass buck naked so as to dissolve any inhibitions Jen had about communal living.

. . .

Jen put on a light blue blouse and navy blue skirt, slipped on a pair of black pumps and walked back to campus for her job interview in the main library. There Miss Lorena McKee Baker, the little old lady head librarian, surprised Jen and her perfect smile by welcoming Jen to the World of Work and hiring her as a page, twenty hours a week at a buck an hour. Miss Baker then summoned a library page named Natasha for an orientation. For Jen's first-ever-in-her-life hour as a member of the Work Force, Natasha made sure Jen understood the Dewey decimal system as well as a page's duties and priorities. She showed Jen the stacks from a library page's point of view: seventeen floors in the throat of the Tower and in which was housed close to a million books. Jen learned to shelve a book the main library way: spine up so the next library page on that floor could check to see it was correctly shelved before placing it spine out. Later, going to get their next hour's assignment, Jen used a Michael A. line on Natasha:

"Sooo what's your story, morning glory?"

"Me? I'm banned from Boston so I'm lost in Austin—got kicked outta Wellesley for my politics. Now I'm floppin' on a couch at *The Rag* office."

"Heady stuff," Jen said, liking this woman with granny glasses and straight black hair down over her shoulders, white peasant blouse, fine long legs in a tan mini skirt and combat boots. "You know what, Natasha? This is turning out to be a truly providential day. It so happens my boyfriend, me and two other guys got a house and there's an extra bedroom. It needs light bulbs but the rent's $20 a month. You interested?"

"Damn right I am."

· · ·

After her two-hour shift at the library Jen met up with Natasha. Now there was an army green medic's bag strung over her left shoulder, a copy of Austin's underground newspaper *The Rag* poking out of it. As they walked down the South Mall, Jen learned more about Natasha.

"I play keyboards," she told Jen. "I got a Vox Continental with a Toby amp. Got it right after hearing Alan Price on "House of the Rising Sun.""

"Cool," Jen said. "My boyfriend and I play guitar."

The women were almost to 200 West 19th when Natasha pointed aloft at a kite with a purple crab design and said, "I hope the house with the kite flying from the roof is ours? Be far out if it was."

"That's us alright," Jen said.

Going up the porch steps and hearing the Monkey Ward's Stereo blaring Cream's "I Feel Free", Natasha's mini-skirted hips began moving to the music. Following Jen through the front door and into the entryway, Natasha gave an approving nod at a small printing press in the entryway. She then grinned at a newly printed sign on the balustrade beside the stairway that said **DEN OF INIQUITY, PROCEED AT YOUR OWN RISK**. Next she saw three guys in the living room. In a purple butterfly chair was Jack trying to figure out the chords to "I Feel Free" on his Mexican guitar. On the faded red couch with a 4'x6' American flag above it were Taj and Michael A. Taj was sitting up straight, Michael A. in a reptilian slouch, rose colored glasses atop his head as he idly scratched his rump while his mouth munched down a mayo and peanut butter sandwich. Each held a *Playboy* opened to the fold-out. At their feet were other *Playboys*.

Due to the blaring "I Feel Free" none of the guys had yet to notice Jen and Natasha. Jen, however, saw that today's purchases of furniture, fridge and stove had been brought into the house only to be left right where where they landed and Jen was pretty sure the two empty quarts of Old Milwaukee Beer were the reason why. Going over to the stereo and switching it off, she said:

"See what I brought, guys."

Right away Jack looked up and, ever bashful, blushed and nodded hi. Taj folded his *Playboy* and grinned sheepishly while Michael A. put his rose colored glasses back on and, leering at Natasha, sounding cheery, said:

"*Welll!* What vision of loveliness and enlightenment have we here?"

"Reinforcements, some gender parity," Jen said. "Natasha's our new housemate." Making introductions next: "My boyfriend Jack, Taj ... and Michael A."

"Too, *too* splendid," Michael A. said, still leering. "You got a guy, Natasha?"

"No guy, but I do have these." Natasha then took the *The Rag* out of her medic's bag and unwrapped it to reveal several light bulbs.

Michael A. grinned and said, "Did Jen mention Nude Tuesdays?"

"Wow," Jack said, holding one of the light bulbs, 'this one's still warm."

"They're recently liberated," Natasha said.

Michael A. said, "Housemates, I sense this woman to be a kindred spirit."

Pointing at the small printing press, Natasha said, "Whose is that?"

"Mine, all mine," Michael A. said. "Might you be in need of a print job?"

"*The Rag* is looking for a new printer due to, uh, political pressure."

"I'm hip and I'm also your man, darlin'. I can print handbills and tickets too."

"You print *tickets*?" Jen said. "As in Lavender Hill Express concert tickets?"

"Just General Admission, Jen," Jack said. "That way nobody gets hurt."

Jen said, "The sign on the stairs is no lie, Natasha—this *is* a den of iniquity."

"Annnh," Natasha said, waving it off while giving Michael A. a wink, "a little larceny's necessary for the revolution."

Jen now pointed at the empty Old Milwaukees and said, "Beer? With so much to do?"

"Beer when*ever*," Michael said, his tone defiant.

Jack said, "We were moving the stove when Michael A.'s back went out." "Old pool table injury," Michael A. said. "Beer gets me up'n running again."

"But no one here is twenty-one," Jen said. "Who bought the beer?"

"Cheepers," Michael A. said. "The house fuzz is busting us jaded heathens."

"Michael A. bought the beer with his fake I.D.," Jack said.

48

"Rat fink. Philistine," Michael A. said. "My own flesh an' blood too."

Now Jen picked up a *Playboy* and opened it to the fold-out. "Methinks Miss February is going to have back problems later in life."

Natasha said, "Do skin rags appeal to your prurient interests, Michael?"

"Not right now—too many worms in the image—and my name is Michael *A.*"

Still looking at the *Playboy*, Jen said, "Your mom let you to have this filth?"

"She's who bought 'em." Taking the *Playboy* to clutch it like a teddy bear. "They're art. I've been collecting them since the eighth grade."

"They're obscene," Jen said.

"Meaningless word, man," Michael A. said. "Supreme Court said so."

"That opinion's been localized," Natasha said.

"Are you C.I.A., Natasha?" Michael A. said. "FBI infiltrating the old college try? If you are, don't tread on me 'cause I'm American as apple pie. Semper fi, hail to the chief an' all like that. You pre law mayhaps? What're you majoring in?"

"Revolution," Natasha said.

"Ouu," Michael A. said. "I do believe I'm getting incalescent."

Ignoring him, Natasha said, "By the way, who's the kite flyer?" When Taj raised his hand, Natasha smiled at him and said, "Right on, brother, groovy to the max. Crabs're cool, the kite kind anyway. Will you show me how to fly it?"

Taj nodded affirmatively and got up to stand beside her.

"I helped him make it," Michael A. said. "I named it the Purple People Eater." Then, as Natasha and Taj started to leave: "Hey? What say we have a Wesson Oil Party to christen our union as soldiers in the struggle?"

"Annnh," Natasha said, waving him off as she led Taj away.

Jen now took Jack by the hand to lead him away, too, saying, "I got a job."

"All reet," Jack said and gave her a Furry Freak Brothers hand-shake.

Jen then looked back to say, "Have fun with Miss February, Michael."

"Michael *A.*"

# CHAPTER NINE

Once the Purple Crab kite had safely returned to Earth, Natasha left after saying she would move into the 19th Street house the next day. The black church door was then placed atop concrete blocks that had been liberated—same as the two hoses filling up the water beds—from nearby Connelly's Florist. Once the black church door became the dining room table and the scratched-up chairs set in place, Michael A. declared he was starving and no one objected when he offered to spring for burgers and fries from the Mooreburger next to Connelly's. No one objected, either, when upon his return, he pushed the Stromberg Carlson to the end of the church-door-turned-dining-room-table so that it was in front of the book case that went all the way to the ceiling. After placing Barney and Thelma Lou in their goldfish bowl atop the TV, Michael A. said it was time to tune in Lady Bird Johnson's KTBC Channel 7 so Taj could watch *The Uncle Jay Show*. Then, while waiting for the tubes of the Stromberg Carlson television set to warm up, Michael A. took the straight back chair at the head of the table and made an impromptu incantation.

"Oh boob tube, black and white fiend, all-seeing eye, awake from your fetid sleep and bless us infidels with your lies an' foolish-ness, your absurd juxtaposition. Oh Keeper of the Vast Wasteland, mind laxative amuck with Barnabas Collins, Uncle Jay, Packer Jack, Wile E. Coyote, Road Runner, Uncle Walter's Evening Blues, load us up with hooey annnd give us *Tuuube Tiiime!*"

. . .

Later, after Uncle Walter had delivered his sign-off of "And that's the way it is, Wednesday, January 3, 1968", the new housemates gathered on the front porch. Jack and Jen were on the top steps, he with his Mexican guitar, she with her Gibson. Michael A. sat holding his bass in the one of the purple butterfly chairs and Taj was seated on the floor reading the headlines of the *Austin Statesman*. With Taj alternately frowning and wincing, agonizing over the local, national and world misery on the front page, Jen started singing "I Feel Free" and Jack and Michael A. joined in. When everybody— including a lip-synching Taj—harmonized the chorus, it amazed them how well their voices blended.

"Cool tune," Jack said. "Be neat to do an electric version. All afternoon I've been getting rock'n roll vibes. Suddenly nothing but rock in my head." Then: "If we formed a band, where would we practice?"

"We could set up in the bedroom next to mine," Michael A. said.

"We'd need band equipment," Jen said.

"Where there's a will there's a way," said Michael A.

"We need a couple more musicians," Jack said. "A drummer for sure."

"Natasha plays keyboards," Jen said. "She has a Vox Continental."

Silence next, nobody saying a word. Then Taj, front page of the *Austin Statesman* still in his hands, clapped his hands together three times so as to make eye contact with the others. Next he began patting out a beat with his right foot and countering it with downbeats from his left foot. Then he began squeezing some of the newspaper's pages like an accordion but it sounded like marimbas.

"Wow." Jack said, "Taj, are you a drummer?"

Nodding enthusiastically, Taj took out his Marks-A-Lot and wrote on the *Austin Statesman's* front page: *Got drum set, will play!*

"Well, whaddya know," Michael A. said, "our Taj *is* an Everyman."

Everybody's attention was now on Taj as he began again with his paper marimbas, alternately tapping his feet to lay down a familiar beat.

"That's 'I Feel Free' alright,'" Jack said. "Hum the melody, Jen, an' you'n me harmonize, Michael A."

52

Everybody got into it: humming then harmonizing, Taj lip-syncing. Jen sang the lyrics with help from Jack and Michael A. and when the song was over, everybody just looked at each other with enlightenment until Jen said:

"I say we rock."

. . .

They were calling it a night. Taj was already in his room, but Michael A. seemed to be lingering. So Jen got a sly smile on her face and said:

"Are you scared to go downstairs, Michael A.?"

"Certainly not. I'm just taking my time because my water bed's not full yet."

"Ours is full," Jack said, sly smile on his face. "Yours should be too."

Jen said it again: "You're scared to go downstairs, aren't you?"

"Why would I be afraid? On account of the bugs?"

Jen straightened and, brow furrowed, said, "*What* bugs?"

Now with his own sly smile Michael A. sang, "*La cucaracha, la cucaracha...*"

"Cockroaches?" Jen said, head turning, looking around. "Infestation?"

"Be cool, hon," Jack said. "You're forgetting Cuz is into dynamic tension."

"Oh," Jen said to Michael A., "so you're just kidding."

Pointing a finger at her, he said, "Yep'n I gotcha good, didn't I?"

"The furies never sleep, spitbird! Say your prayers to Mona the ghost!"

"Beep-beep," Michael A. said and went downstairs.

Jack and Jen now looked at one another, glad to be alone. "We did good, huh, hon?" Jack said. "We got us a place to live."

"Yes, our karma's good right now," Jen said. "We're embarking on another transforming experience, crossing the threshold into another chrysalis."

"What's 'chrysalis' mean?"

53

"A stage of being, or protected growth." Then Jen paused before saying, "Do you think this place is haunted?"

"Be kinda cool if it was." Then: "Michael A. sure gets to you, don't he?"

"Little bit." Wincing her nose.

"But you still like him, don't ya?"

"Not much." Making a face. "I bet when he was a kid he ate his boogers."

"Like I said, he's impish and a stinker. But he's also a damn fine bass player ... and he can sing."

"Yeah, he can play bass and sing, I'll say that for him—but that huge collection of *Playboys* is demeaning to women."

"Awww, he only has 'em 'cause he likes their cartoons."

"But that dynamic tension bit and those annoying nuances are too—"

"He's my cousin, Jen. It was him carried me out to the Big Bend in a '66 white T-Bird'n helped me'n Nacho dig Granpa's grave. He's also my best friend."

"Well, if he's your best friend, what am I?"

"The woman I love and adore and want to spend the rest of my life with."

"Really? Honest?"

"Durn tootin.' Cross my heart an' hope to die."

"Well then don't I get a say about Michael A.?"

"Sure seems like it you been getting your fair share. I just wish ..."

"You just wish what?"

"That, well, that you'd lighten up some on that particular topic."

"He's a hipster doofus. A jive ass creepy womanizer, a twisted satyr who irks the crap out of me." Then: "So there. I'm done ... for today anyway."

"You just wait, the guy will grow on you."

"Frankly I worry he'll grow on me on 'cause he's probably infested with something." Then, thinking of Kilroy: "Did you say a '66 white T-bird?"

# CHAPTER TEN

Taj was glad that no one had wanted the rear upstairs bedroom. It pleased him to have a north view from his twin-sized mattress on the oak floor because the view was the University's skyline. The view of the Tower particularly seemed to speak to him. He wondered if this was perhaps because it reminded him of the minarets atop mosques during his time in the Middle East. What was even better about the rear upstairs bedroom, however, was that it also had access to the roof. It was the roof where Taj intended to spend much of his time.

Now, lying in his bed and looking out at the Tower, Taj's mind pictured what he had seen up on the roof while flying his Purple Crab kite. He was picturing the roof itself, his mind's eyes scanning it when his attention came to rest on the large red brick chimney near the middle of the roof. His mind now fixed on this large chimney, and this last image made him frown.

Because he had not seen any fireplace in this old house.

. . .

Jen's mother—not the June Cleaver one—had told her daughter it was a man's world but that it was a woman's bedroom. "Now listen here, young lady," she would say after she had had a few, "don't use that furry thing you sit on to do a guy who puts perk in your girdle—use it to land yourself somebody who can put a roof over your head, food in your tummy and a nice car to drive to the country club. Even better'd be two weeks every summer in the Rocky Mountains and charge cards for Cox's, Leonard's and Monnig's." Jen was recalling of this mom-daughter chat as she lay on the water bed and said to Jack:

"Jack be nimble, Jack be quick."

55

"I'm working on it, Jen, but these Lucchesses're awful tough to get off."

Teasing, Jen said, "My psych prof said a guy should name his penis."

"What in the world for?" Boots and jeans off now, getting into bed.

"Because a guy should be on a first-name basis with what makes most of his decisions." Next Jen got a devilish grin on her face as she took said subject in hand. "So how about we name this big fella 'Cowboy?' That okay with you?"

Voice down an octave, almost breathless, Jack said, "Yes, ma'am."

"Great." Then, devilish grin even bigger: "So where's your hat, Cowboy?"

. . .

In their first mail delivery at 200 West 19th Street Jen got a letter from her father forwarded from Helen M. Kirby Hall. Just the sight of it sent anxiety creepy-crawling through her, a worse dread than the thought of a kajillion roaches she feared were lurking somewhere in her new home. For long, agonizing moments she stared at the letter but could not bring herself to open it. She wondered if it was a suicide note. Or a confession. Whatever it was she could not yet handle, so she stuffed the letter into her now irrelevant Estee Lauder makeup bag then went to Gregory Gym to stand in line to register for classes.

. . .

For the spring semester of 1968 Jen's fifty-minute classes on Mondays, Wednesdays and Fridays were with Joe Maloff, Patricia Kruppa, Roger Abrahams and James Ayres. On Tuesdays and Thursdays she had Joe Kruppa's Electronic Media class for ninety minutes. Not coincidentally, Jack had the same classes.

Natasha mentioned only Larry Caroline's philosophy class.
Taj?... Who knew?
Michael A.? Who cared?

56

Michael A., never cut out to be a pleasant presence like Taj, always seemed to find a way to make his presence known to his house-mates. For one thing, he was a finicky eater. When Taj served up the first communal meal of couscous as the main course then substi-tuted fruit for the meat and vegetables over the steamed cracked wheat and called it dessert, Michael A. nearly had a cow. The second night Jen made a rice pilaf that Michael A. barely touched and she caught him making a barf face when he thought she was not look-ing. The third night Natasha made "Revolutionary Pie," something that looked like a cross between a cheese pizza and a Swanson pot pie sans chicken or turkey or any flesh whatsoever—but Michael A. choked that down. The fourth day an unprepared Jack boiled some Oscar Meyer weenies at the last minute and set them on the church-door-turned-dining-room table alongside a loaf of Mrs. Baird's White Bread and bottles of mustard and relish. Weekend meals were Grab As Catch Can.

Michael A. had also become adamant that Mona the ghost lived downstairs and thus he had yet to spend a night down there. Every morning found him disheveled and with a galloping case of bed head while sprawled out on the faded red couch, his uncom-monly ugly toes sticking out from beneath an army blanket—not a pretty sight as everyone but Taj had to go past him on the way to the kitchen. One afternoon, as Jack and Jen and Natasha and Taj sat around the church-door-turned-dining-room-table clipping coupons from the previous Sunday's *Austin American Statesman* for double coupon Wednesdays, they heard Michael A.'s motorcycle pull into the garage. A moment later he stormed into the kitchen then stomped into the dining room to set a bag of Mooreburgers on the church-door-turned-dining-room-table. Right away Jen teased him, saying:

"How's life downstairs with Mona the ghostie, Michael A.? She still there?"

"Check," he said. Then: "But never mind Mona—I got a plan that'll make enough moolah not only to score us band equipment but also make Kash Karry double coupon Wednesdays unnecessary. A plan to kick off our rock band and"—looking at Taj—"put good ol' American fried, baked, grilled meat on our table."

Giving him a suspicious look, Jen said, "You're talking about a scam, right?"

"A scaaam? Moi?" Pointing a finger at his heart while winking at Natasha. "Certainly not. This innovative idea of mine is completely on the up'n up. Even a notoriously cynical non believer like you, darlin' Jen, will attest to its brilliance."

"Let's hear it," Jack said, starting to grin conspiratorially as he turned to Jen and said, "It can't hurt to listen."

"Don't be too sure of that," Natasha said. "In today's Amerika just listening in can be construed as hatching up a conspiracy."

"No conspiracy—I've merely been pondering pithy pearls of wisdom."

"You mean scams," Jen said.

Ignoring her, Michael A. said, "It has come to my attention that students can reserve, free of charge, any auditorium on campus."

"So?" Jen said.

"What ya got in mind, Michael A.?" Jack said.

"We'll show movies'n make a bundle of moolah—how's that sound?"

"Flicks?" Jen said. "What flicks?"

"Feature films," Michael A. said. "Flicks are sure to draw a crowd."

"Let's get *The Graduate*." Jack said. "That's a good'ern."

Taj wrote on his small white vinyl clipboard then held it up: *Camelot*.

"Or *Marat/Sade*," Natasha said, getting into it. "Up the revolution!"

"I'm hip," Michael A. said. "All good choices, but, alas, alack … no. Our debut feature presentation shall be a famous foreign art film."

Natasha said, "Fellini's La Strada? Anthony Quinn's a huge SDS supporter."

"Ingmar Bergman's *Wild Strawberries*?" Jack said.

"Neither," Michael A. said. "Though *Wild Strawberries* is close as our flick is also Swedish. No, we have latched onto what may be the Motion Picture Association of America's first ever X-rated film."

"*I Am Curious(Yellow)*," Jen said. "We just talked about it in Kruppa's Electronic Media class—it's pure titillation." Making a face as she said to Natasha, "A girl kisses a guy's you-know-what in it."

"A *sex* film?" Natasha said while giving Michael A. a look of disgust. "A piece of sexist trash that demeans and exploits women?" She then got up and headed for her room, saying, "I want nothing to do with this."

Michael A. said, "But it's got an interview with Dr. Martin Luther King."

"Male chauvinist pig," Jen said to him.

"Darlin', if you weren't Cuz's only ever girlfriend, I'd—"

"You'd what, pig?" Teeth bared, ready to let the fur fly.

"Look"—softening his tone—"sex sells. The take will be huuuge."

"Aw, simmer down, you two," Jack said. "I wanta hear more."

"Whoa!" Jen said to Jack. "Are you going along with this sicko's scam?"

"I support free speech," Jack said to her. Then: "You gotta projector, Cuz?"

"It comes with the auditorium. I've already put an ad in the *Daily Texan*."

"But who'll run the projector?" Jack said.

Taj raised his hand.

"Good ol' Everyman," Michael A. said.

Jen said, "So just where are you procuring this, uh, art film?"

"Good ol' Uncle Tunoose."

"Family rate of course?" Jen said.

"Natch. He'll even throw in the sequel, *I Am Curious(Blue)*."

Jen said, "Is this another communal living deal? An even Steven split all around? If it is, I think I can convince Natasha to go for it."

Michael A.'s response was to grin like a banshee.

. . .

Besides the ad in the *Daily Texan*, Michael A. printed handbills and
Jen and Natasha put them up on campus bulletin boards. Jen had to
go into the R.O.T.C. Building alone, though, because Natasha said
the only way she would go in there was with a Molotov cocktail.
On Friday evening, January 12, Purple People Eater Productions
charged $1.25 admission—25 cents less than Congress Avenue's
State Theatre or Paramount—and raked in $432 from an Academic
Center Auditorium's showing of *I Am Curious(Yellow)*. $100 went
to Uncle Tunoose and the rest was split six ways: a share for each
house member plus another for a kitty kept in a Castor Oil bottle
that Taj had found in a closet.

"Fat city" was how Jack termed it.

"Seed money" was Jen's term.

"Too bad we can't sell popcorn," Michael A. said.

"Yet one more Capitalist pig rip off through the exploitation of
women," was Natasha's summation. Then she shrugged and said,
"But a girl's gotta eat."

The next Wednesday, double coupon day at Kash Karry, they
bought eighteen boxes worth of supplies, a larder of victuals which
they hoped would keep them provisioned well into the spring
semester. Now the shelves in the kitchen pantry were stacked with
family size jars of Peter Pan Peanut butter, Bama Red Plum Jelly,
Bama Grape Jelly and Bama Peach Jelly, Libby's Sweet Gherkins,
Libby's Dill Pickles, Libby's Sour Pickles, French's Mustard, Miracle
Whip, Heinz Ketchup, Thousand Island Salad Dressing, French
Dressing, Wesson Oil, Aunt Jemima Pancake and Waffle Syrup.
There were cartons of Grapette, Orange Nehi, Coca Cola, Big Red
Soda, RC Cola, Dr Pepper. Cans of Folger's Coffee, Austex Chili,
Vienna Sausage, Van Camp's Pork and Beans and Ranch Style
Beans. There were family size boxes of Cheerios, Captain Crunch,
Sugar Crisp, Kix, and Rice Crispies. There was a giant-size box of

Bisquick. There were Hostess Cupcakes, Twinkies, Oreo Crème Sandwiches, Fritos, Cheetos, Lay's Potato Chips and pretzels. There were loaves of Butterkrust Bread, Hot Dog Buns and Hamburger Buns. There were rolls of Mr. Whipple's Charmin toilet paper. Other paper products included Dixie Cups, paper towels and paper plates—Michael A.'s choices for three of the twentieth century's greatest inventions because he did not have to wash them. The Hotpoint fridge was full of 39-cent Old Milwaukee Beer, six packs of Lone Star beer, Superior Dairies Homogenized Milk, Kraft's American Cheese Slices, Minute Maid Orange Juice, Extra Large Grade A Eggs, Nestle's Quick, Bosco, Ovaltine and Parkay Margarine. Below the kitchen sink was Fab detergent, Chlorox bleach and Joy dish washing detergent, Bab-o, Bon Ami, Mr. Clean, Lysol cleaner. Above the sink was Pepto Bismol, Alka Seltzer, Tums, Carter's Little Liver Pills, cod liver oil...and Lavoris mouth wash.

The Hotpoint fridge's freezer, of course, was stacked high with Homemade Vanilla Blue Bell Ice Cream, one of which held the communal baggie of pot.

Still, Natasha and Jen did their best to make available fresh fruits and vegetables and salad makings. Also, Jen was talking of learning to use the Neiman Marcus yogurt maker she had bought as her parents' Christmas present.

Michael A. and Jack still made bottle runs like the one Jen had witnessed back at Helen M. Kirby Hall in September, 1965. Nowadays the reason behind such pilferage was to underwrite Michael A.'s turn to provide a meal. On those days the 19th and University kids either went to Lavaca Street for El Toro Number Two Dinners or down on the Drag for steaks at the Night Hawk, lasagna and Chianti at Victor's Italian Restaurant or Sixth Street to the Hoffbrau or Caruso's where Natasha got as many oysters as her heart desired once Michael A. learned from Taj that they were thought to be an aphrodisiac—though so far it was nothing doing with regard to Michael A.'s aim of bedding the revolutionary. All this eating out courtesy of Michael A. every fifth day did not last long, however, for one day Michael A. and Jack returned from a bottle run empty-handed. When Natasha saw this, she looked up from reading Mao's *Little Red Book* and said:

"What went wrong, guys? Unexpectedly thwarted in your thievery? Or—perish the thought—were you busted?"

"Nope, none of the above," Jack said. "They've stopped using glass bottles in vending machines. These days it all cans."

"And you can't make a dime off cans!" Michael A. screamed.

"Cool Breeze knows how," Natasha said.

# CHAPTER ELEVEN

Though much to Michael A.'s dismay there were no Nude Tuesdays, Scantily Clad Sundays were unavoidable. Michael A. would read *Playboy* while lying on the faded red couch wearing nothing but his BVDs. Or, after having taken a chance with Mona the ghost on a downstairs shower, he would come upstairs with only a Villa Capri towel wrapped around his waist. Once outside Natasha's bedroom door he would serenade her with The Guess Who's "American Woman", belting it out with verve and flair while gyrating hips a la Elvis until he lost his towel.

Then early on the morning of Super Bowl Sunday, January 14, 1968, Michael A. woke up the household by playing The Doors' first album full blast on the Monkey Ward's record player. As Jim Morrison moaned and groaned and gave Oedipus a run for his money in "The End," Michael A. lay on the faded red couch wearing nothing but a fearful countenance, his uncommonly ugly toes curled up and out from beneath his army blanket. A look of abject fear was on his face, his eyes were dilated and bloodshot and his hands trembled as he tried to read a *Blackhawk* comic book. On the floor in front of the faded red couch were two empty quarts of Old Milwaukee and copies of *Look, Life,* and several *Playboys*. The loud music brought everybody out of their rooms to see a hand scribbled sign attached to the stairway's balustrade. The sign said ***Ghost. Phantom! Spirit! Ghoul? Specter? Poltergeist? Banshee? HAINT!*** At first everyone looked at it each other and then at Michael A. as they shuffled into the living room. Jack was barefoot in his number 69 maroon and gold Alpine High Fighting Bucks football jersey. Jen wore her white baby doll pajamas and white sweat socks. Natasha had on her combat boots and a sheet. Taj looked dapper in a gold silk bath robe and cordovan brown opera shoes. When Jen shut off the record player, Jack, rubbing the sleep from his eyes, said:

"What's up, Michael A.? Why all the racket?"

"Bad trip?" Jen said.

"Acid flashback?" said Natasha.

Not a peep out of Michael A., just a fearful stare. So Natasha tried a Florence Nightingale: going over to him, putting a hand on his wrist and saying, "What's the matter, honey? Pussycat got your tongue?"

"I got a huge case of The Fear—a Haint sang to me."

" 'Haint?' " Jen said. "What's a 'haint'?"

"A ghost," Jack said. Then: "What did the haint sing, Cuz?"

" 'I Know You Rider.' "

"Cool old song, we gotta do it," Jack said.

"You sure it wasn't roaches?" Jen said, her eyes examining the floor.

"A haint," Michael A. said. "She's out to get me. I can't take it no more."

Natasha said, "So we got a ghost—must we do this on a Sunday?"

"She came up here and tried to get me—I almost snapped."

"You're positive it wasn't roaches?" Jen said. "It wasn't roaches, was it?"

"Nope—death was upon me. Pure umber horror"—wincing—"in a pale nightgown."

Natasha said, "I'm surprised a MCP like you didn't try'n jump her bones."

Jack frowned and said, "What's a 'MCP'?"

" 'Male Chauvinist Pig'," Jen said.

Michael A. said to Jack, "I was right, Cuz—death is a woman."

"Really?" Jen said. "Who was it last night? Daphne? Lenore?"

Jack, grinning now, said, "Or Gail? Barbie? Barbara? Liz? Pam? Elyssa?"

"Really, guys", there's a ghost down there."

"No more *Dark Shadows* for you, Cuz," Jack said. "You can't handle it."

"*Dark Shadows* has vampires," Jen said, "not ghosts."

"Ghosts, vampires, the boogieman," Natasha said, snickering. "What a wuss." Taj next placed his hands at the sides of his forehead, index fingers pointing upward, causing Natasha to say, "Yeaaah, it was the devil, that's who it was." Then: "Come on, Michael A., it is most uncool to wake us up on a Sunday morning with demonic rock 'n roll just to put us on."

"Well, it sure wasn't Broadway Joe Namath comin' up the stairs—I almost came unglued. Look at Barney 'n Thelma Lou—they're scared spitless."

Everyone now turned to look into the dining room at Thelma and Barney Lou in their goldfish bowl atop the Stromberg Carlson TV.

"They're fine," Jen said. "They're not freaked out."

"Desperate guys tell desperate lies," Natasha said. "*Lame* lies in this case."

Jen said, "Yeah, it was just a ruse to soften up Natasha."

Everybody then headed back to their rooms. But Natasha paused at her door just long enough for Michael A. to say to her:

"Honest injun, darlin', something's downstairs an' it's out to get me. Can I at least sleep on your floor? I'm scared to be alone at night in this house."

"Bunk with Taj."

"He snores."

"You're lying—he sleeps in the next room and I'd hear him."

"Oh, please, Natasha, pretty please? I'll be good, really I will. I promise to respect and honor you every moment."

"Annnh," she said and went into her room slamming the door behind her.

But, never one to worship a woman from afar, from that morning on Michael A. wooed Natasha. From in front of her closed door he would either get down on one knee, hands over his heart and profess his eternal love or he would carry her books to class then wait outside like some faithful dog. He took her for picnics on the South Mall. He fed her tuna fish sandwiches from his Judy Jetson

65

lunch box and gave her Big Red soda from the thermos. He bought her a dozen yellow roses from Connelly's Florist and had them delivered with cards on which he had written "Has the curse been lifted yet?" and "How do I love thee? Let me count the ways" and "Baby, I'ma want you" and "Wild thing, I think I love you."

And Natasha responded. She let him take her to Green Pastures for a romantic dinner then dancing later at the Sheraton Crest. Natasha even eschewed her combat boots and wore pumps so she and Michael A. could gracefully glide across the dance floor like a pair of Peggy Flemings on ice. And Jen could not believe it, much less stomach it. So she got Natasha off to one side and said:

"My god, girl—what on *earth* for?"

"For reasons you'd never suspect. Politics makes strange bedfellows. He's afraid of the dark and I'm not, so he needs me."

"Propinquity?"

Natasha considered this for a moment and said, "He's a hard man to shed."

"It's his 'dynamic tension' shtick, isn't it? Plus you're lonely an' life's short."

Natasha shrugged then, deadpan, said, "Yeah, that too … but mostly it's the wooing and all the wining and dining...he's sweeping me off my feet."

And then, when that morning that Jen so dreaded came to pass, when she came out of her bedroom to find Michael A. exiting Natasha's room, humongous Cheshire cat grin on his face, all Jen could do was grimace and shake her head then say:

"I hope she urps all over that Mount Rushmore you have for an ego."

"Ouu, just a wee-eensy-wispy thread of irony there," he said then stuck his tongue out and said, "Dynamic tension, darlin'— works ever time."

. . .

On Friday evening, January 19, the showing of *I Am Curious(Blue)* netted the 19th and University kids a profit of $498. The following

66

Tuesday afternoon they piled into the Fitty Six, Jack and Jen and Natasha up front, Taj and a much chagrined Michael A. relegated to the shiny yellow pickup's bed for the drive to Strait Music Company next to the S&H Green Stamp Redemption Center at North Lamar and Tenth Street. There, using the $498 as a down payment, they went into debt: for Jen a blond Fender Telecaster, for Jack a red Gibson Melody Maker and for Michael A. a brown hollow body Fender bass. For amplification they got a Fritsch Public Address System with four microphones and four microphone stands, two Fender Super Reverb amplifiers for Jack and Jen, a Fender box for Michael A. plus a fuzz box and wah-wah pedal for Jack and an echo box for Jen. For Natasha, Michael A. bought a harmonica and a tambourine.

Taj, meanwhile, bought himself a cow bell.

# CHAPTER TWELVE

Saturday morning, January 20, Dylan's "Masters of War" on the juke box, Jack was at the usual Chuck Wagon table reading the *Daily Texan*. "It says here," he said as Michael A. took a seat, "casualties in Vietnam for 1967 were 9378 dead which is up from 5008 in '66."

Michael A. dug into his bowl of peaches, gulped some of his half pint of Superior Dairies Homogenized Milk and, mouth full, said, "Did they use that new word in the American lexicon—body count?"

· · ·

Monday morning, January 22, Jack and Michael A. were again in the Chuck Wagon, Jack once more reading the *Daily Texan*, the juke box playing Buffalo Springfield's "For What It's Worth" when Jack said, "It says here the commies just made a surprise major attack on a place called Khe Sanh."

"Hmmm," Michael A. said as he opened his half pint carton of Superior Dairies Homogenized Milk. "Could be things are heating up over there. If the body count keeps going up, the big brass will request more Gook fodder, more of what they call 'boots on the ground'—us."

"So?"

"So I'm gonna see some low friends in high places about some life insurance."

· · ·

Friday evening, January 26, Purple People Eater Productions pulled down $312 for a Batts Hall Auditorium showing of *Dr. Strangelove Or How I Learned to Stop Worrying and Love the Bomb*. The following Tuesday, January 30, Jen came home upset from being unable to coax a traumatized dog from beneath a parked car. By the time she made Jack go back with her the dog was gone. Next it was off in the Fitty Six to Town Lake Animal Shelter to adopt pups, a brown male and a white female. On the way home, Jack driving north on Lamar, the dogs in Jen's lap, getting petted more than at any time in their lives, Jack said:

"The male is kind of coyote-looking, so let's we call him Wiley."

"Okay," Jen said, "and we'll call the female Beep Beep."

Jack laughed. "How come you think the Road Runner is a female?"

"Do you agree the coyote's a male?"

"Yes, ma'am, sure do."

"Then the Road Runner's a female."

"How come?"

"'Cause all those silly cartoons symbolize the male pursuit of the female."

"Nawww, the coyote's just hungry—he's hunting the Road Runner."

"He symbolizes a man chasing a woman to the point of losing his dignity and slipping beneath himself—same as Michael A. keeps doing with Natasha."

"Aw, Jen, please don't ruin *The Road Runner* cartoons for me."

"Awww" Jen said, "Is Cowboy down? Is he pouting?"

"*Cowwwboy* ain't got nothin' to do with it." They were now turning off North Lamar to head east on 19th Street. "And quit petting those dogs so much— they're not poodles or terriers or any other lap rats—they're just dawgs."

Giving Jack that certain look now, Jen said, "They need to see me as their mother figure. Otherwise they might run out in the street and get run over."

"'Mother figure?' They're dawgs. They bark if someone comes around an' they bite 'em if they get too close. That's how it works with outside dogs."

"I wasn't allowed to have pets as a kid, Jack. I just had dolls."

"What's that sposed to mean?"

"It means I want to keep the dogs in the house."

"I'll teach 'em to mind so they won't run out in the street."

"Have you taught me to mind yet, Jack?"

"Now cut it out, Jen. Nobody's callin' you a dawg."

"Bet I can be a bitch if I put my mind to it. Just ask Michael A."

"Let's leave Michael A. out of this."

"Wiley and Beep Beep can be housebroken and they'll learn to mind."

"I don't know how to housebreak dawgs. It's just ain't done where I come from. 'Sides, they'll get up on the water bed an' rip it open with their nails."

"We'll clip their nails."

Frowning now, Jack said, "They'll chew up the furniture."

"That's no biggie in our house." Then: "Jaaack?"

"Whut?"

"Are we having our first fight?"

Jack sighed. "Course not. I'm just trying to prevent infestation is all … and you know how you feel about infestation."

Now it was Jen who frowned. "What's infestation got to do with it?"

"Them goldurned dawgs is gonna bring dirt'n fleas'n ticks in the house."

Jen shook her head. "This is different."

"Bugs is bugs, Jen—how in the world is this different?"

"Because these dogs are going to be our babies."

"Lawsy mercy," Jack said and fumed to himself until he had pulled into the driveway, parked in the garage and turned off the ignition. Then, giving Jen a stern look: "I'm gonna have to put my foot down about this dawg situation."

"Like hell you are. We'll hold a house council and vote on it."

. . .

That night at dinner Natasha made what she called "slumgullion with Russian dressing." When Michael A. got a gander at it beforehand, he lit out for the Kash Karry and bought quarts of 39-cent Old

71

Milwaukee for the guys and Mateus wine for the gals. After dinner Michael A., again at the head of the table, made a toast.

"To success, to crime," he said, raising his quart of Old Milwaukee.

Jen, giving Jack a feisty look as she gave Wiley and Beep Beep bites of slumgullion, then held up her Dixie cup of Mateus and said, "Here's to plain speaking and clear understanding."

Natasha said. "Power to the people—right on!"

Next Taj gave a power salute of solidarity but all Jack did was grit his teeth.

"We shall now vote on some house rules," Natasha said.

Right on cue Michael A. said, "Rule Number One: If you're not there, you don't get any."

"All in favor raise your hand," Natasha said.

Everybody raised a hand but Jack.

"Rule approved," said Natasha and looked at Michael A. who took another gulp of Old Milwaukee and said:

"Rule Number Two: If you leave it, you lose it."

"All in favor raise your hand," Natasha said.

Everybody but Jack raised a hand.

"Rule approved," Natasha said and looked at Michael A. who took another gulp of Old Milwaukee and, wincing, eyes closed, said:

"Rule Number Three: Underwear for women optional, required for men."

"All in favor raise your hand," Natasha said.

Once again everybody raised a hand but Jack.

"Rule approved," said Natasha and again looked at Michael A. who took yet another gulp of Old Milwaukee and, giving Jack a look of pure pity, said:

"Rule Number Four: Dogs run free."

"All in favor raise your hand," Natasha said.

All raised a hand but Jack who said to his cousin, "Ratfink. Philistine."

Michael A. shrugged this off with, "Hey, man, it was bigger than both of us, peace in the sack an' all like that." Next, whispering to Jack: "She douches with Lavoris—what more could a guy ask for?"

Which was when Natasha, now glaring at Michael A. like she would bite his head off, said, "Rule Number Five: only the one who cooks sits at the head of the table. All in favor raise your hand."

Everybody raised a hand but Michael A. who frowned mightily as he clenched his fists and said:

"Leapin' Lizards! Foiled again."

Taj now wrote something on his small white vinyl clipboard with his Marks-A-Lot and held it up for all to see: *House rule #6: No public displays of affection*

After exchanging looks with Jen, Natasha said, "All in favor raise your hand."

And Rule Number Six was approved by everybody but Jack and Michael A.

. . .

Tuesday, January 30, in the Chuck Wagon, Barry Maguire's crusty voice singing "Eve of Destruction", Jack was reading the *Daily Texan*. "The North Vietnamese an' Viet Cong've attacked a hunnert cities 'n towns in South Vietnam," he said to Michael A. "They even occupied the U.S. Embassy in Saigon for eight hours."

Michael A. said nothing, just drained his half pint of Superior Dairies Homogenized Milk.

"They're calling it the Tet Offensive—are you worried about your dad?"

"Why should I?" Michael A. said. "He's never worried about me."

"Are you worried about getting shipped off to Vietnam?"

"That's not me, man. I ain't gonna be just another leaf blown away by that big wind called the draft. Uncle Tunoose's is gonna cover my ass."

"How?" Jack said. "He gonna get you a draft card sayin' you're 4-F?"

"Nope. What he's got in mind is even better."

Jack's eyebrows shot up in surprise. "You're movin' to Canada?"

"Nope, I'm playing dead for this war." Then winked. "Uncle Tunoose's gonna get me a death certificate."

73

# CHAPTER THIRTEEN

By February, 1968, the 19th Street house had begun to thrive. It had become a place full of laughter, a little yelling, some sheer exuberance and Michael A.'s dynamic tension. Until bedtime all doors were open, the housemates digging their unity and celebrating their idealism. Bring it on but easy does it for life is short; this much they knew. Also the house took on a more lived-in look. In front of the tall window in the living room were terra cotta pots of plants, ferns and philodendrons—plants Connelly's Florist had relegated to the alley only to be recycled by the 19th and University kids. In the kitchen window sat a pot of ivy started from a cutting from Mrs. Dr. Kruppa. From Ma Bell's North Lamar maintenance lot wooden spindle spools were liberated and what once had held heavy gauge wire now held the Monkey Ward's Airline record player or served as lamp tables beside the water beds. Above the faded red couch was the American flag. Wall posters were here and there: on the north wall of the living room was a poster of Che Guevara's posed corpse in Bolivia; Andy Warhol's Campbell Soup Can was on the wall in the dining room next to the book case that went all the way to the ceiling; Marlon Brando on a motorcycle from *The Wild One* was above Natasha and Michael A.'s water bed; over Jack and Jen's water bed was James Dean with his thumb hooked in his jean pockets plus Jane Fonda—and her wonderfully long legs—in her Barbarella outfit; the 1967 Be In held in San Francisco's Golden Gate Park adorned Jack and Jen's bedroom door. Spray-painted in pink on what was now Natasha *and* Michael A.'s bedroom door was **Den of Iniquity, enter at your own peril**.

Taj's room was minimalist to the max: zero, nada, zip, just his twin-sized mattress on the floor, a jar of peyote buds beside the bed, a tensor lamp aimed at the wall and a rope ladder leading to the roof. His orange Motorola transistor radio was usually on the window sill. The *Austin American* hitting the front door was how Taj awoke every morning.

This had been how Taj had found the kittens.

· · ·

The Language of Touch was now heard frequently in the 19th Street house, mostly late at night or early in the morning or all during the weekends. Michael A. even seemed to bring his dynamic tension approach to the bedroom in the form of vocal foreplay. He would go to the door of his and Natasha's bedroom, open it then stand there with a look of stunned admiration before saying:

"Splendid, darlin', utterly *splendid*. Starting' without me, are ya? Don't move a muscle, I'll be right with you. Wanta tickle first? A pinch perhaps?" And then Natasha's voice could be heard saying in her direct tone of voice:

"Use it or lose it, wuss."

Whereas behind the closed doors of the front bedroom was a kinder, gentler issuance of the Language of Touch. For instance Jen would let out a low moan of pleasure sounding like "*Uuuummm*" which would make Jack stop what he was doing and say from beneath Nacho's gift of a red handwoven wool blanket from Palenque, "What's the matter, Jen? Can't talk?"

"Don't stop, please, don't stop," Jen would say breathlessly, her hands reaching down to take Jack behind the ears. "Pussycat got your tongue goood."

# CHAPTER FOURTEEN

February, 1968. The Vietnam War was worsening and the tide that was America's youth was rising, steadily swelling against it. The war's numbers did not lie. Call them casualties or body count, they were taking their toll on good old American can-do optimism and widening the credibility gap between the government and America's youth. For draft eligible young men like Jack and Michael A. the *Daily Texan's* headlines were Chinese water torture: each new day brought another drop of dread about whether or not they would be thrown to the lions. Stay in school or go maim, kill somebody, possibly die. Even those back from Nam had lost part of themselves over there. Be it part of their body or their mind, these wounds never healed. And the women worried about their men. As Natasha said:

"We who stand and wait still serve."

But in the 19th Street house there was the boon of hope and the joy of love. The 19th Street kids were having a ball even if the world around them was going to hell in every headline. On Friday, February 2, Purple People Eater Productions showed Alfred Hitchcock's *Indiscreet* at the Academic Center Auditorium and made a profit of $432. The rest of February's Friday nights would also be Hitchcock: *Suspicion, Saboteur* and *Shadow of a Doubt.*

On top of that there was the music: it sweetened the 19th and University kids' lives by cultivating their creativity, inspiring and sustaining their self-esteem, let them feel not only super alive but follow their bliss via one sound, one voice.

The band itself, however, was getting off to a slow start. They practiced in the living room but there they flopped around like fish out of water working up Jen singing lead on "I Know You Rider" and Natasha singing "Gimme Some Lovin."

77

Jen's assessment was, "We suck like schmucks."

"You said it, darlin'," said Michael A.

So Natasha put forth the notion that band practice should be treated as a "rite of solidarity" and held downstairs. By doing so, she reasoned they would be isolated, no distractions from the outside world. Michael A. objected, avowing that the 'haint" down there would not like it, that all their loud and as yet lousy rock and roll would drive Mona up a wall. But when Natasha pointed out that the music would be muffled down there, thus lessening the possibility of noise complaints and thus visits from the "pigs", Michael A. got on board. So the hand scribbled sign saying: **Ghost. Phantom! Spirit! Ghoul? Specter? Poltergeist? Banshee? HAINT!!** was removed from the top of the stairway and their new band equipment was taken down there.

It became an inner sanctum they called the "White Room."

The White Room proved to be a catalytic ambiance. In the White Room they slowly started feeling *their* way until the *band* began to feel *its* way. From the start Taj was the stable focus that a drummer should be. He could either lay down the beat or elevate it, whatever was needed. Meanwhile, Michael A.'s bass added texture and thus bass and drums complemented each other well enough for the rest of the band to have a firm foundation to play on. Initially, Jen and Natasha sang the leads without any harmonizing from the others. Then Jack, Jen and Natasha started singing the chorus of "House of the Rising Sun" and this brought in a nuance that Michael A. felt he could embellish so he joined in the chorus as well. With no one having early morning classes they became more nocturnal with regard to their music: they started late and played late just like they would if they had a gig. They shut themselves in the White Room and at midnight, a candle burning beneath the black light, they would gather in a circle on the floor to sit Indian style while holding hands and harmonizing, even Taj lip-synching along until they got it right. They set a goal of six songs, maybe a half hour's worth of music, and from then on they began putting it to themselves until they believed they were average, not good, but they did not stink, either.

"We got potential," Jack said.

"We could play frat rat parties right now," Natasha said.

"We still suck like schmucks," Jen said, and Michael A. would say:

"You said it, darlin'."

In time they got six songs down well enough to please, first, Jen and then Michael A. who said he would start casting about for a gig. They still lacked a band name and also promotional photos for prospective clients, but they had their six songs: "I Feel Free" plus Cream's version of Robert Johnson's "Crossroads", "I Know You Rider", "House of the Rising Sun", the Zombies "Song of the Season" and The Spencer Davis Group's "Gimme Some Lovin'."

"So we just keep on keepin' on?" Jen said to Michael A. after the practice down in the White Room when they decided they were ready to play in public. "Is that what we do, Mr. Ways and Means?"

"Nope, first we'll throw us a bash an' party hearty with our pals."

"Yea! A party," Jen said as Jack nodded approval.

"Parrrrteee," Michael A. said.

"Parrrteee. Parrrteee," said Natasha and then Taj began a rhythmic clap, mouthing the word, everyone joining in, harmonizing:

"Parrrrteee. Parrrrteee. Parrrrteee."

. . .

Jen's old pal from the Nu Mus, Jolinda Biggs used Jen's 35 mm Pentax to take the band's promotional photos. It was hazardous work, too, for Jolinda had to fend off Michael A. who was unable to control himself: eyes fixed on Jolinda's chest, his lust for her bodacious bosom so overwhelming he kept up a nonstop patter:

"Do they have names? Do ya use 'em as water wings at Barton Springs?"

"You lay a hand on me," she said, "you'll be wearing it around your neck."

"I can't help it," he said, "I'm starstruck." Then to Jack: "Get a load of those puppies, willya? It's like the mother ship calling me home."

The day of the band's photo shoot the 19th and University kids also got themselves a boost up in The Fine Art of Hanging Out, courtesy of Uncle Tunoose, who sent over a super duper television antenna. Though Natasha put it down as a talisman of the leisure class and goose-stepped around the dining room chanting "The revolution won't be televised, the revolution won't be televised," she and Jen were voted down in a house vote, Taj providing the swing vote. Once Taj had lashed the super duper antenna to the chimney the Stromberg Carlson TV picked up three San Antonio stations plus stations in Waco and Temple. That first day the TV was on from three in the afternoon until midnight when all channels went off the air with the singing of the national anthem over an American flag background. From then on Jack and Michael A. were in hog heaven. Besides *The Uncle Jay Show* and *Dark Shadows*, now Tube Time included reruns, cartoons, soap operas and sports. In the afternoon it was *The Life of Riley, The Adventures of Ozzie and Harriet, It's a Great Life, Make Room for Daddy, The Three Stooges.* At dinnertime it was still Uncle Walter delivering the evening blues but afterwards became Theatre in the Raw. Michael A. would act like a big shot emcee by tapping his Dixie cup with his dinner knife, saying, "Attention, boys and girls, it's time for *The Rocky and Bullwinkle Show.*" In the evenings it was *Rowan and Martin's Laugh In, The Red Skelton Show, The Jack Benny Program,* San Antonio's Channel 12 for news—they had the most violence—followed by *The Johnny Carson Show.* Saturday morning it was cartoons and *Boston Blackie, Captain Midnight, Sky King, Fury,* more sports in the afternoon followed by *Marlin Perkins' Wild Kingdom, Saturday Night at the Movies* and *Shock Theatre.* Sunday mornings, after sleeping in and reading the *Austin American States-man,* it was sports until dinnertime when they watched *The Walt Disney Hour.*

The downside was when Michael A. smoked pot he would go on massive fooders. Also, Jack spent less time in bed with Jen, studying and otherwise. Jen wished that the Stromberg Carlson would die via Planned Obsolescence.

But TV did not keep Taj from his roof access. By now the Purple Crab kite was being maneuvered to above Cambridge Tower on 18th and Lavaca.

In spite of it all, though, the band practiced every night from midnight on.

And whenever they played "I Know You Rider" or "House of the Rising Sun" a vague shadow seemed to darken the black curtain of the White Room's only window, causing the blood to drain from Michael A.'s face.

. . .

Though life was busier, more cramped, it still went on. It was classes and the Chuck Wagon, classes and work at the library. Because library pages had to get their hourly work assignments from a clipboard on Miss Baker's desk, it gave the old gal a shot at them. Jen and Natasha were not accustomed to a sweet little old lady with a wisecracking sense of humor who, when she saw Jen or Natasha not wearing a bra, would say, "I see ya got your high beams on, honey." Or for a tight skirt and no bra: "You're wrapped tight enough, dearie, but tied loose." Jen would just show her perfect smile and flow with it but Natasha would say:

"Social revolution starts from daily life."

But what Jen and Jack and Natasha and Taj loved most was the solitude of the library's stacks. Handling and being around so many books—a million of them it was said, some of them not checked out in fifty years—seemed to suit them. They liked the library's eccentricities, too. There was the book elevator, a dumbwaiter that delivered books to all sixteen floors. There was the Snead, a vertical conveyor belt that brought books requested by undergraduate students to the fifth floor to be checked out. There was the pneumatic tube system in which the undergraduates' book request forms were placed in a plastic tube then pneumatically sent flying up or down to the page working on the floor nearest to the requested book's location, a bell announcing its arrival. Taj showed off his practical joker side by either using his Marks-A-Lot to write graffiti like

81

"Beware hand gobbling snakes" next to the plastic tube's arrival station or curling himself up in the book elevator and riding it to the floor Jen, Natasha or Jack was working and, when they opened its door, Taj would roll out like a dead body coming out of a trunk in an old timey mystery movie. There were interesting surprises tucked away in the library, too. Like the "Z" Room on the third floor, where bound volumes of Victorian era smut written by English nobility were kept as well as modern erotica like *The Story of O* and off-the-wall novels like William Burroughs' *Naked Lunch*. There were also the complete writings of Harry Houdini that supposedly could only be checked out by a member of the Magicians Society, though a lowly library page would be entrusted with the key and thus pour over this forbidden fruit.

Then there were the graduate students who had been assigned study carrels in the stacks. The carrels were similar to monk's cells in a monastery: small desks separated from the adjacent carrel by a five-foot high partition with book shelves attached to hold the research material a graduate or post graduate student relied upon to complete his or her thesis or dissertation. Some of these grad students could turn into weird characters after being shut up in the Tower for a whole semester in a dark place where talking was frowned upon. Sometimes this dungeon-like environment produced pranks to relieve the pressures they were under and often times a library page was an easy victim. Jen nearly freaked out one day when, while shelving a book, she came upon a psychology grad student hanging by the neck from the light fixture over his carrel, tongue hanging out, eyes bulging, only to drop the act before Jen completely lost it.

When he tried it on Natasha, though, she laid him low with a well-aimed combat boot to the groin.

# CHAPTER FIFTEEN

February 12, Lincoln's birthday, was a Monday. That evening the Gamma Sigs were on the front lawn of their red brick house on the south side of 19th Street, the frats drunk and hootin'n hollerin' at the traffic going by. On the north side of the street Taj, Jack and Jen were up on their roof. Taj, with a mischievous smile on his face, was showing Jack and Jen a laser gun he had borrowed from the Engineering Lab. In 1968 lasers were known by the masses as death rays in science fiction films while real ones could only be found in university engineering labs and were supposed to be used only for scientific purposes.

As soon as Jen saw Kilroy—pie-eyed of course—she made Taj show her how to use the laser. Next she zapped Kilroy with a red spot, keeping it on him as he freaked out, began flailing away wherever the spot was on him while yelling:

*"It's on me! It's on me!"*

As Kilroy's fellow frats wailed the daylights out of him, a smiling Jen was saying, "Kilroy got it there...and there...and there."

. . .

On February 14, Valentine's Day, a Wednesday, Jack took Jen to Victor's Italian Restaurant at 29th Street and the Drag. At a candlelit table with a red and white checkerboard tablecloth they had a bottle of Chianti, dinner salads and plates of lasagna plus all the baskets of garlic bread they desired. During dinner Juan, an unappealing young man with mutton chop sideburns, dark hair parted in a hard line and slicked down with Brylcreem and wearing a long-sleeve white shirt with black bow tie and dark trousers, came over with a violin to play something romantic. Though Juan was awful,

Jen pretended to swoon. When Juan left a buck richer to play the same tune for another couple, Jen leaned forward and said:

"Jaaack?" Batting her eyes and giving him that certain look. "In psychology I learned romantic relationships have three phases: lust, love and companionship. Which one do you think we're in?"

Jack did not miss a beat. Right away he said, "Why all three, of course, but I don't think we'll ever leave the love phase."

"Awww, that's so sweet," Jen said, swooning for real now.

. . .

For Valentine's Day Michael A. took Natasha to Hill's Steak House on South Congress Avenue despite Natasha insisting that she was not in the mood for a hunk of mangled animal carcass. Their waitress was an overly plump fortyish bleached blonde with more makeup than Giggles the Clown and wearing Wrangler jeans, a red, white and blue western shirt and black cowboy boots that made her wince when walking. Michael A. ordered porterhouse steaks, baked potatoes and iced teas. He requested his steak well done and served sizzling while Natasha wanted hers "blood red, no sizzle a-tall." As their waitress waddled off wincing, Michael A. said:

"My love, sweet mystery of my life, darlin', where does your woman's intuition see us next year on Valentine's Day, 1969?"

"Locked up."

"Why? What're we gonna do? And where will we be doing it?"

"We'll be down at the Capitol."

"Protesting or marching?"

"Neither. We'll be throwing Molotov cocktails at that fascist Connolly."

"But you say we're gonna get locked up an' that's not revolutionary it's—."

"Martyrdom," said Natasha. "We'll be martyrs."

Michael A. sighed and said, "Ohhh, what a revoltin' development this is."

. . .

Valentine's Day for Taj meant that he had the house all to himself, so he decided to find where the chimney was located within the house.

. . .

Michael A. called Jack and Jen's king-sized water bed the "Lust Nest." But, mostly, when not studying each other's anatomy and eloquently attending to the Language of Touch, Jack and Jen would study together there, Wiley and Beep Beep wrestling on the floor or snoozing peacefully when not wagging their tails whenever Jen looked their way. And Jack was wrong about the dogs getting on the bed—they could not handle the unstable footing.

On the other hand, Natasha and Michael A.'s bedroom was as advertised: a Den of Iniquity for often these lovers were degrading the Language of Touch into the Lingo of Lust. So much so that even Miss Baker at the library would notice the strawberry-sized hickeys on Natasha's neck and say, "Hope you gave as good as you got, honey." Or, during Tube Time commercials, Michael A. would point out the scratches on his forearms and say to Jack with a prideful grin:

"Ya oughta see my back—looks like I got raked over by a pitch fork."

Jack would then raise his eyebrows and say, "You sure you didn't?"

All too often Jack and Jen and Taj's attention was drawn to the sound of shattering glass followed by hearty, vigorous moans and groans, mild yelps of pleasure or pain, thumps and humps, slaps, giggles, spanking and downright dirty low whimpers interspersed with muffled yelling and screaming. Once when this weird foreplay had ceased and the water bed in Den of Iniquity could be heard moving rhythmically, Jen lowered her assigned reading of John Updike's *Rabbit, Run* for Dr. Ayres modern American novel class and said to Jack beside her:

"What's the difference between screaming and yelling?"

Brightening, Jack said, "Is this a psychology assignment?"

"Easy, Cowboy, I'm in search of the truth is all."

"Hmmm," Jack said, "Is screaming passive voice and yelling active voice?"

"Ouu, impressive thinking. Methinks you've a future on the planet."

Jack then did his Elvis impression: "Thank ya, thank ya very much."

Next, hearing a duet of orgasmic vocalization in Den of Iniquity, Jen said, "Methinks the harmonizing in the White Room is causing side effects." Hearing this, Jack believed he was being given a hint, so he took *Rabbit Run* from Jen—only to have her put up a mild protest, saying, "As you were, Cowboy, I gotta read that by tomorrow to get a good grade."

"Good grades're overrated, hon." And then from Den of Iniquity came:

"What do we do next, my panting, pulsating revolutionary?"

"Whatever your imagination allows, whomp dog."

"The water bed's about to boil over'n my baloney pony's been rode raw."

"Far out—now we scorch the earth. Get your scrawny honey buns over here and I'll show you the other side of this life. I'm gonna knock your block off, ya big stiff, but first I'm gonna stand you on your horny head and—"

"Ouu, yeaaah—Kama Sutra Position Number Sixty Nine, right?"

There then followed a cacophony of grunting, sighing, gasping, the sound of skin slapping skin and some of Michael A.'s signature yelps as their king-sized water bed went on its own stampede. But none of this weird foreplay or whatever behavior that ensued was paid any attention by Jack and Jen because back in the Lust Nest, Jen was bending low over Jack's chest to kiss him deeply then rise up and squeeze him hard as she said:

"I gotcha surrounded, Cowboy."

. . .

February 22, a Thursday, was Washington's Birthday. It was late in the evening and Taj was again on the roof of the 19th Street house. On his face was an impish smile and in his hand was the laser. Over at the Gamma Sig house it was quiet as most frats were down on the Texas-Mexico border for "GWB in Laredo."

But there were still a few brothers on the premises.

One of which was Kilroy who was half in the bag and and nipping at his flask while leaning on one of the front porch's white pillars. When Taj saw a cat sniffing around a garbage can on the frat house's east side his impish smile turned mischievous. Aiming the laser so the cat could stalk it, Taj moved the laser's red spot slowly toward Kilroy. The cat wanted to pounce but Taj kept the red spot out of reach. Across the front lawn of the house the red spot and the cat went, onto the walkway leading up to the house. Kilroy now saw the red spot heading for him, the cat in hot pursuit. First, Kilroy flung his flask out onto 19th Street where it bounced off the pavement on the lawn of 200 West 19th Street. Next, the red spot and the cat now racing up the Gamma Sig steps toward him, Kilroy freaked out and did a lolling, swerving hundred-and-eighty degree turn to bolt for the frat house's front door. Kilroy's dash to a safe haven was thwarted, however when the red spot got him between the shoulder blades. The cat, claws flared in attack mode, then leaped onto Kilroy's red-spotted back.

Once the hysterical screams had subsided and a weeping Kilroy was in the Gamma Sig house being cared for by brothers, the cat went back to sniffing the garbage can and Taj came down from the roof. Now in stealth mode so as not to disturb the two Language of Touch dialogues being carried out in the other two upstairs bedrooms, Taj went from his bedroom via its west door into the dining room. From the dining room into the living room Taj tiptoed into the entryway, a finger on his lips to shush Wiley and Beep Beep. He then went outside and onto the front lawn to pocket Kilroy's flask while saying:

"Finders keepers, losers weepers."

. . .

87

It was Thursday afternoon, February 29, warm enough for Michael A. and Jack to bring the purple butterfly chairs out to the front porch, church-key-open a quart of Old Milwaukee and kill time before *The Uncle Jay Show*. Both had one thing on their mind: the moment in the White Room the night before. The moment came when the band sat Indian style on the floor holding hands while harmonizing "I Know You Rider" and the White Room's one candle flickered then went out.

"Mannn," Michael A. said, "when that candle went out all of a sudden that gal of yours could sing."

"Yep," Jack said. "Zippo bang zoom'n she could sure enough sing alright."

Michael A. took a pull on the quart, gave it to Jack. "She's transformed."

"Yep," Nodding. "She says so too. She said she was transformed down in Palenque too, so I guess women are just more spiritual than guys."

Reclaiming the quart, Michael A. said, "What the ghost angle?"

"Come on, man, your Super Bowl Sunday 'umber horror in a pale nightgown' bit was pure bull, a line for Natasha. You don't believe in ghosts."

"Maybe I do. I've been under a great strain lately. See, I didn't tell all of what happened when I moved in downstairs. Yeah, I heard stuff, a moan, a groan an' maybe it was the wind, the house settling or a critter moving around and, yes, it's true that nothing came upstairs to get me that Sunday … but there's other stuff that went down that could get me butterfly-netted … an' nowadays I hear hummin'n ouuin' whenever we do 'I Know You Rider' an' 'Rising Sun'."

Taking the quart, Jack said, "What other stuff?"

"No way, not a word. Might be cool for a guy like you who was raised with a ghost lover like Nacho—but I wasn't raised like that an' seeing's believing … an' what I've seen' is wayyy too much of… somethin'."

"A 'vague shadow in the corner'."

"Check. An' during' 'Rider' there was something on the black curtain behind Jen flickering to the beat. So I'm wondering if it wasn't Jen's voice but … ?"

"Whoa! Jen has a ghost's voice? A ghost nobody but you even senses?"

"So far, but it's gettin' scarier'n scarier down in the White Room."

"What's Natasha's take?" Chuckling. "Something revolutionary?"

Michael A. said, "Well, she's sure not blowing it off like you are."

"Hey, I'm not into busting a gut about anything. I just deal with what is an'"—taking a pull from the quart—"go with the flow or else get out of its way."

"Yeah, yeah, Mr. Lead-Follow-or Get-Out-of-the-Way." Then, taking back the quart for another pull: "But back to Natasha—she thinks it has to do with last midnight kicking off the extra day in leap year."

"What's February 29th's got to do with ghosts?" Taking the quart back. "It's 'cause music inspires us, takes us to a higher level an' Jen's just feeling' it."

"It's getting to be like a séance down there In the White Room."

"Somethin's happenin,' what it is ain't exactly clear … but I like the results."

"We're getting' there, we're definitely feeling' it. I'm diggin' it, so's Natasha. She's starting' to play around on the harmonica, wants to do "Spoonful." Grinning now, Michael A. said: "Course I'm helping' her on that mouth organ, teachin' her to play the slobber blues on my meat whistle."

"You dawwwg." Finishing the beer, Jack said, "I gotta question."

"Lay it on me, Cuz."

"Does Natasha wear those combat boots in bed?"

. . .

Friday, March 1, Purple People Eater Productions made a profit of $444 from showing Hitchcock's *The Man Who Knew Too Much* at the Academic Center Auditorium. For the rest of March's Fridays

they planned to show Bogart movies: *Treasure of the Sierra Madre,
The Maltese Falcon* and *Casablanca.*

. . .

At noon Saturday, March 2, Texas Independence Day, Taj had just
named his spot on the roof the "Crow's Nest" when the Gamma
Sigs traditional firing of their old-timey cannon set Wiley and Beep
Beep to howling for a whole minute.

. . .

Jack was scanning the *Daily Texan* at the 19th and University kids'
table in the Chuck Wagon while pretending to listen to Jen. The
Doors "Break on Through to the Other Side" was on the juke
box when Jack read that, according to the *Texan*, LBJ had barely
beaten anti war candidate Senator Eugene McCarthy in the New
Hampshire Democratic primary, that the U.S. command was claim-
ing an infliction of more than 500 enemy casualties at some place
called My Lai, that Robert F. Kennedy had entered the race for the
Democratic party's presidential nomination and that LBJ's military
advisers had urged him to end the war.

In the meantime Jen was blabbering a blue streak about Joe
Kruppa's class—the one Jack had cut today—and how exhilarating
1920s Paris must have been with the Dada movement's "happen-
ings" put on to show the Dadaists' opposition to bourgeois values.
Jen went on to say that in Mrs. Dr. Kruppa's class—which Jack had
cut yesterday—she had learned that Christmas being on December
25 was only a political ploy against another religion whose leader
was born on December 25. Jen next launched into a tirade about
how she had been raised not to come out and touch a man because
it was wrong and unwanted, but now she had decided that this was a
load of hooey and it was okay to feel up a guy. When Jack heard Jen
say she wished he would quit acting like her father and stop reading
the paper while she rambled on like some nagging dumb bunny, Jack
looked up from reading about Congress repealing the requirement
for a gold reserve to back U.S. currency, and said:

90

"Trust yourself, be honest and true."

. . .

The evening of March 31, the thirty-sixth president of the United States of America, Lyndon Baines Johnson, was addressing the nation on all three major television networks. In the two story red brick house at 19th and University LBJ was on the black and white Stromberg Carlson television set saying, "My fellow Americans" when he was overridden by Michael A. saying:

"Hey, hey, LBJ, how many kids did you kill today?"

"Shut up, I wanta hear this," said Natasha.

As soon as LBJ wound up his address by saying, "I shall not seek and I will not accept the nomination of my party as your president" Michael A., brow furrowed, said, "What's that mean, darlin?' What's he saying?"

"He's saying he's a sick and tired old man who can't hack it anymore."

"Dayum! The tide's turning an' we're gonna get out of this Vietnam mess!"

"No way. The military industrial complex has too much money at stake."

After giving this some thought Michael A. said, "You know, they say if you call the Kremlin you can listen to a recording of the entire communist manifesto."

# CHAPTER SIXTEEN

Mother Nature was once again inspiring the rebirth of life via her incipient sigh: spring was happening. Mornings had become an operatic cheeping of birds. Austin's trees were greening and flowers domestic and wild were reaching up to the Capital City's blue skies. On the green grass of the South Mall dogs were chasing Frisbees, soap bubbles were being blown, cutoffs and tank tops were ubiquitous, harmonicas and recorders were being played and under South Mall trees lovers were cooing to one another and holding hands and sneaking kisses.

Love was in bloom at 19th and University, too. In the evenings Jack and Jen often took *Analuz* in the Fitty Six down to Town Lake for a spin. On the water a hatch of snapping turtles seemed to cover every rock and all creatures on water and land were going with the flow, going along to get along, riding the tide of spring's rebirth.

When not scorching the earth in the Den of Iniquity, Natasha and Michael A., could usually be found at the church-door-turned-dining-room-table. On a typical evening Natasha would do Michael A.'s nails or some other form of topical hands-on activity. Upon Jack and Jen's return from Town Lake, Jack and Jen would gaze forlornly at Michael A. and Natasha being so cuddly-snuggly and Jack would say, "Hey, Jen, you think you could do my nails?" And Jen would say, "Nope, just keep biting them." Michael A. would then get a glib grin on his face until Natasha would dump the hand she had been working on and stand up to go around behind him, bend over and give his left ear a wet willie. Jen next would bring up House Rule Number Six—no public displays of affection—whereupon Natasha would walk away with an exaggerated wiggle in her butt, Michael A. slinking along right behind her saying, "Darlin', do I ever have a good half foot of Mexamerileb sausage for you." And Natasha would say:

"That teeny eensy weensy weenie? That little bitty ol' thing? Again?"

"Awww, I can barely walk an' you wanta cut me off at the knees."

"Okay, c'mon an' lessee what ya got for me."

· · ·

As the Austin weather grew warmer, most afternoons Jack and Michael A. turned into porch lizards. Jack would sit in Granpa Gage's bentwood rocker idly playing his guitar while Michael A. was plopped in a purple butterfly chair and seemingly without a care in the world. On the top step of the front porch a hibachi would be grilling decaying animal flesh and it and the smell of pot smoke would bring Jen out to see what was going on. To Michael A. in his pith helmet, wraparound shades, unlit Pall Mall in his mouth, safari shirt, jodhpur britches and combat boots with purple and yellow argyle socks, she would say:

"Tacky, Michael A., mighty tacky." Then, frowning at Jack in his Hawaiian shirt and boxer shorts: "As for you, Ben Jack Gage, you're lying around too much drinking beer'n rotting your teeth on chips'n day-old Mrs. Johnson donuts."

Jack's sly-grin-reply was, "Is it a good day for a cayuco ride, hon?"

"Oh hell yeah it is—you're on."

# CHAPTER SEVENTEEN

"Someone's eyes must greet the dawn," Jen said, thinking of Nacho as they stood by *Analuz* admiring a peregrine falcon gliding above the Rio Bravo on a norther.

It was Tuesday, April 2, Spring Break '68 and the lovers were a mile south of Terlingua ghost town. Jen had never seen Jack's "Big Empty", had never been humbled by such a stark landscape, such a colossal sky. There was not a tree anywhere, but there were blue mountains here at the tail end of the Rockies. With the norther at their backs ruffling their long hair and buffeting their jeans and jackets, they looked at the Rio Bravo from a rise in a field of knee-high Big Bend Bluebonnets. Jack and Jen stood together arm in arm, hip to hip, leaning on one another. From here the mouth of Santa Elena Canyon to their right was less than a mile away and Big Bend National Park began a few miles east, its Chisos "Ghost" Mountains in full view from Mule Ears Peaks to Emory Peak to Casa Grande. Nearby Granpa Gage was interred beside his wife, son and daughter-in-law overlooking the river he had called his "big muddy buddy what's too thick to drink and too thin to plow." His simple grave was a mound of river rock adorned with a garland of Big Bend Bluebonnets that Jack and Jen had put below the wooden cross of driftwood carved with Granpa Gage's name, dates of birth and passing. Jen's cheek was nestled into the hollow of Jack's shoulder as he clasped her to his chest.

"Jaaack, why're the mountains blue?"

"I don't know, hon, but I'm looking into it."

"There's a plastic Jesus on the dashboard of the Fitty Six."

"I know it. I hope the pump jockey in Marathon'll take it when we get gas."

Wednesday, April 3, Jack was having a 15-cent french-fry brunch in the Chuck Wagon. The jukebox was playing Donovan's "Season of the Witch" when he saw in the *Daily Texan* that Ho Chi Minh said he was ready to discuss peace.

Thursday, April 4, 1968, Uncle Walter was on the Stromberg Carlson saying, "At 6.01 p.m. at the Lorraine Motel on Mulberry Street in downtown Memphis, Tennessee, Dr. Martin Luther King was shot" when Jen began crying, weeping openly for a good man. Jack could only shake his head and comfort Jen. Michael A. said even a cynic like himself did not see the assassination coming. Natasha bowed her head and swallowed hard then looked up at the ceiling before bowing her head again, seeming to pray. Taj looked at all of them then stood up and walked away. That night in the main library Taj used his black Marks-A-Lot to write on the "Z" Room wall: *the white race is a cancer on human history.*

Friday, April 5, Purple People Eater Productions showed *High Sierra* in Batts Hall Auditorium and made a profit of $428, all of it given to the National Association for the Advancement of Colored People.

Saturday, April 6, to honor Dr. King's there was a march for solidarity on 19th Street. In the march were Dr. Roger Abrahams and plenty of sympathizers and mourners like Cool Breeze and the 19th and University kids. Ignoring Natasha's sneer of "It'll never happen", Michael A. told everybody that Austin should name a street after Martin Luther King. Jack and Taj stayed up all night in the White Room working on a song about the horrific event of April 4, 1968.

Wednesday, April 10, the 19th and University's Stromberg Carlson showed the Academy Awards Presentations. The Oscars went to *In the Heat of the Night* for best picture, its star Rod Steiger for best actor and to Kate Hepburn for best actress in *Guess Who's Coming to Dinner*. By now the King assassination had sparked riots killing 46 people in Baltimore, Boston, Chicago, Detroit, Kansas City, Newark, Washington, D.C. and elsewhere.

On April 11 President Lyndon Johnson signed into law the Civil Rights Act..

April 12 Purple People Eater Productions showed *Nosferatu* at Batts Hall Auditorium for a profit of $412. That night Michael A. was banished from Natasha's bedroom. Mona's moans then sent him from the faded red couch out into the driveway where Cool Breeze was just arriving in his pink Cadillac. The boys then went partying until dawn at Charlie's Playhouse and the No Tell Motel.

# CHAPTER EIGHTEEN

Michael A., recognizing that things were heating up on the planet, suggested that the band take their harmonizing to the dinner table and make it a house custom to raise their Dixie cups after the Nightly Blues and say, "One world, one planet."

The first night they did this Michael A. was invited back into Natasha's bed.

The band was getting there, everybody said so.

And most of them were giving the credit to Mona the ghost.

Now, when they shut themselves in the White Room and sat in the dark Indian style in a circle on the floor around one candle to hold hands and practice harmonizing, Jen, too, felt that the candle flickered to the beat and that Mona was singing along through her.

Natasha now swore that Mona lived in the downstairs bathroom and liked the music so much she was dancing the Watusi in the black curtain.

Now, whenever Michael A. entered the White Room, he talked to Mona in the space next to him, chattering away as if she were beside him. Jack's reaction was to give Michael A. look of pure pity and say:

"*Bulll!*"

. . .

Tuesday afternoon, April 16, Jen was saying to Jack, "How come you missed class again today? Kruppa lectured about absurd juxta-position in 20th century media."

"'Cause it was my turn to make dinner."

They were in the kitchen. Jack was slapping together hamburger patties and liberally salting them until Jen took the salt shaker away from him ans set it on the counter. Fists on her hips, she said:

"It's a ninety-minute class—it doesn't take *thaaat* long to make burgers."

"No, it doesn't, not when ya got the makings, which I didn't. I hadda go to Kash Karry'n get the butcher to give me the good stuff not that fatty crap."

"Seeing as how Natasha won't touch meat anymore, how come you aren't making something that everybody will eat?"

Jack frowned. "Since when don't she eat meat?"

"Ever since her Valentine's Day porterhouse with Michael A."

"Nobody tells me nothin … but Natasha knows the rules an' it's cook's choice so I choose burgers a la Gage."

Jen paused, measuring her words before saying, "You know you really shouldn't be missing so many classes, Jack. You're gonna fall so far behind that you'll be lost for final exams."

"There's more at UT these days than classes. There's tons more going on."

"Like *The Cisco Kid* and *The Lone Ranger*?"

"Naw. This afternoon I learned a new blues run on my guitar."

Jen sighed and said, "Maybe you and I are an absurd juxtaposition. Maybe you're the *CBS Evening Blues* and I'm a Geritol commercial for tired blood."

"I'm don't getcha."

"That's because you don't know what absurd juxtaposition is." Silence next, a long pause until Jen let out another sigh and said, "Fine. Never mind."

. . .

Saturday, April 20, Wiley and Beep Beep showed their dislike for Michael A. when he opened the screen door to the front porch and bent over to swipe Taj's *Austin American Statesman*. Man's best friends nipped at his argyle socks then bit into the hem of his Bermuda shorts and held on for dear life.

100

"Goood doggies, goood instincts," Jen said as she listened through the window of her and Jack's bedroom.

"He's my cousin," Jack said. "Michael A. is family."

"The bad blood in your family worries me, Jack, it really does."

Later that day while his four housemates were working at the library and Michael A. had to pet-sit, Wiley and Beep Beep tested their pet-sitter: they sat dog style by the Stromberg Carlson staring intently at Thelma and Barney Lou in their fishbowl on the book case that went all the way to the ceiling. Michael A. then came in from the kitchen, left hand balancing a paper plate loaded down with a baloney sandwich stacked high a la Dagwood amidst a pile of chips and Libby's Sweet Gherkins, right hand holding a quart of Old Milwaukee. Seeing the dogs' menacing pose at his own pets, he sighed and said:

"Okay, you guys, I get it—it's 'feed us or you'll devour my children."

But Michael A. did not share his sandwich with Wiley and Beep Beep.

No, it was leftover couscous for the canines of 19th and University.

Which right away had Wiley barfing and Beep Beep producing a whopping pile of yellow dog poop and therefore urp and doodoo duty for the Mexamerileb.

"Author! Author!" Michael A. called out with a mighty wince as he bent over to scoop up dogs' the leavings with the paper plate.

For this effort Wiley and Beep Beep awarded him a double butt munch.

. . .

At the stroke of midnight that Saturday it was San Jacinto Day, the day in 1836 when Mexican Emperor Antonio Lopez de Santa Anna surrendered to General Sam Houston after being defeated at the Battle of San Jacinto. Taj was again on the roof looking out on a busy night in the Capital City. When Taj saw a pair of Gamma Sigs exit their frat house and go to the corner of 19th and University, Taj sensed they were up to no good. And Taj was right: they were

hotwiring what Taj knew to be Kilroy's 1966 white Thunderbird.
Soon they were roaring off in it, tires squealing west on 19th Street.
No biggie, Taj thought, but good for a giggle. Then for the next
couple of hours Taj watched a cop car parked in the alley to the west
of Connelly's Florist stake out the red light at 19th and the Drag.
During this vigil Taj witnessed the cops net at least half a dozen
offenders—all young—for either running the light, speeding, or
illegal turns. Twice Taj had seen the guys joy riding in Kilroy's 1966
Thunderbird drive by the Sig house hooting and hollering, each
time having added more fellow conspirators.

Before midnight, as Taj watched an ambulance fly by, siren
screaming, no doubt heading for Brackenridge Hospital on 15th
Street, Taj mouthed the words "Ask not for whom the siren screams,
it screams for you." This was when he saw Kilroy come out the front
door of the Sig House to sit on the front steps and begin drinking—but not from his flask, from a Dixie cup. Taj was wondering
how long it would take Kilroy to tumble to the fact that his car had
been stolen when he reached into his jean jacket to pull out Kilroy's
lost flask and have himself a nip.

"Ummm good, not bad Welch's Grape Juice," he said to himself.

Taj was screwing the cap back onto the flask when he saw Kilroy
leap up, do a double take where his T-bird should have been then
run back inside the Sig house. Taj next saw the cop car in the alley
stakeout turn on its flashing red gumballs and step on it in screaming pursuit of a vehicle on Lavaca. Taj then looked down Lavaca to
see Kilroy's T-bird stopped at the red light at Lavaca and 18th, see
eight guys doing a Chinese fire drill: running around Kilroy's car
while screaming like banshees. But the driver had left Kilroy's white
T-bird in gear and thus it began rolling slowly forward through the
red light, there to be broadsided by a W.O. Harper Plumbing van
just as the cop car screeched to a halt. Next the cops arrived with
guns drawn and made the frats assume the position.

So Taj toasted Santa Anna with a sip of Welch's from Kilroy's
flask.

. . .

102

Sunday morning, April 21, Michael A. charged out the door of Natasha's bedroom wearing only a pair of white athletic socks and purple boxer shorts. Using his momentum, Michael A. glided across the entryway's slick oak floor and flung open the screen door. On the front porch, he wheeled to close the screen door before Wiley and Beep Beep could rush out of Jack and Jen's bedroom.

"Not so fast, you flea-bitten, couscous-pooping butt munchers," he said. "I am the god of hellfire an' today I got your number."

As Wiley and Beep Beep watched, Michael A. swooped up the *Austin American Statesman* then said to the dogs, "As the god of hellfire I bring you—"

It was at this moment that Michael A. felt a twinge, an itch in his crotch, one that made him look down, put a thumb in the elastic waistband of his purple boxer shorts and pull out the waistband for a peek. Slowly it dawned on him what was causing the feeling down there. His reaction plunged him into a deep frown, made him pause for a long, sickening moment before saying in a much lower and much subdued voice:

"Crap! The god of hellfire has brought you ... *gulp!* ... crabs."

· · ·

Sunday mornings had become Jack and Jen's favorite time together. That morning Jen felt Jack's eyes on her and this roused her from her sleep to see Jack resting on his left elbow, gazing upon her with moon dog eyes as he said:

"In repose you are a jewel to behold and I worship you for it and give grace for the blessing of knowing you—you damned sure ain't no pincharita, hon."

Jen smiled through her diminishing dream sleep and arose to go into what passed for her boudoir: stacked fruit crates from Big John's House of Crap that also served as their hippie-style clothes dresser. Jack, meanwhile, placed his arm behind his head to rest it on the wall and admire Jen as she let down her long tresses to begin her morning ritual of combing it out with a hundred strokes from her mom's heirloom brush. The sight of Jen in her boudoir made Jack wonder if the attraction was so strong because as a toddler he had seen his mother in such a scene. From his perspective of lying there in their water bed Jen's long hair became a waterfall shimmering in slow motion, the light through the east windows turning her tresses into tumbling rainbow twinkles like those he had so often seen dissolve into fading reflections amidst cascading rapids in Santa Elena Canyon. Later, when Jen came back to bed and had snuggled beside him, was refreshing herself with the Language of Touch, Jack could only utter a low, erotic moan and put his hand over hers and say, breathlessly:

"You've got my whole world there in your fingers."

And in that moment of tenderness it had not mattered to Jen that Jack was drunk and high and had been up all night making music in the White Room. She had merely leaned in close and over him and said:

"Time to ride 'em, Cowboy."

"Yesss ma'am," he said even more breathlessly, "you're *onnn*."

. . .

Not fifteen minutes later Jack was pulling the Fitty Six into the small parking lot of Raymond's Drug in the 2800 block of Rio Grande just as Michael A. was pulling out of the parking lot on his burgundy Triumph 650 motorcycle. Michael A. had on his rose colored glasses, a T-shirt with a front that said *Who farted?* and between his legs on the Triumph's seat was a brown paper bag. Jack braked to a halt in the Fitty Six, left arm cocked at the elbow and resting on the bottom of the driver's side window as he leaned his head out and said to his cousin:

"You here to cash a check? Gonna buy us breakfast at the Night Hawk?"

"Not exactly." Voice low, not normal. "What brings you here?"

Jack grinned. "I got to buy a hat for Cowboy."

"Right. Of course. Sunday morning in the Lust Nest. Should've known."

Pointing at the brown paper bag between Michael A.'s legs, Jack said, "What ya got there? New plugs? It that time of the

104

month again? Death before dishonor? Tampons and Trojans before Pampers?"

"We'll talk about it later." Then he gunned the Triumph and rode off.

. . .

By noon Michael A. was seated at the head of church-door-turned-dining-room- table and waiting for his housemates to exit their bedrooms. Around the church-door-turned-dining-room-table he had set out a meal from the Chicken Shack at North Lamar and North Loop: honey-dipped fried chicken, Cole slaw and french fries, Dixie cups of Big Red. As his housemates began to file glumly into the dining room, each holding one of the bottles of A-200 from Raymond's Drug left by their doors, he did not visibly react to their baleful glares. But when Natasha pole-axed him with a withering white hot death glare, he attempted humor.

"Attention, boys and girls, welcome to Itchycoo Park." Then stopped because he could tell his housemates were having none of it. So, electing to try to appeal to their sympathy, he said in the quietest tone of voice he could muster, "Look, guys, what we have here is a failure to—"

"Be faithful," Natasha said, setting her A-200 bottle down hard on the table. "You have exposed us all to venereal disease."

"Infestation," Jen said, also setting her A-200 bottle down hard.

"Cuz, you soiled the nest," Jack said, shaking his head.

Taj then made an exaggerated production of holding his nose.

"You're right, Taj, the situation stinks," Michael A. said, his voice now as humble as he could manage. But seeing that not even Taj was moved, Michael A. reverted to humor again, saying in a lighter tone: "Any questions? Conniption fit, anyone?" No reply just dead-eyes glares from everybody, so Michael A. now imitated Henny Youngman doing Ed Sullivan by clasping his hands together, smiling like Cheetah the Chimp and looking around the audience as he said, "Ladies and germs, right here on our stage we have—"

"A self-involved ..."

"Jaded …"

"Self-indulgent …"

Taj's comment was a prolonged raspberry.

"Hey, I'm sorry," Michael A. said, "but I'm only human and you know flaws and foibles are in these days. But fear not, my fellow housemates, for this A-200 stuff will, uh, clear things up." Then he paused to look at their sullen faces—save Natasha's white hot death glare—and deem the situation not down the tubes yet. With a tired shrug, he said, "Imagine my surprise when I found those little boogers crawling around in my pubes. I was appalled. *Shocked* I tell you." When that did not get him slapped, he said, "I must have come in contact with those pesky little critters via a diseased towel in Gregory Gym after my daily calisthenics regimen—an honest mistake that any one of us could've made in these pestilent times. Can't we get past it and enjoy this nice meal which I have provided as a gesture of empathy? We could discuss something more positive. Like coming up with a name for the band? Eh, brothers and sisters?"

Natasha said, "You almost certainly have given me the crabs, spitbird."

"Okay, so I'm Public Enema Number One, a crying disgrace to my own kind. But I'm being up front, aren't I? I'm coming clean." Sounding defensive, eyes blinking as he said, "When there's dirt to be done I'm the guy, but let me get a wee eensy snitch dirty … and maybe you guys might, just might get a little dirty too—welll, then it's hup, two, three, four, kill the messenger … guess I'm just help-lessly hedonistic, a stinker. I'm—"

"A bourgeois centaur," Natasha said. "Now cool your bull before I bust out bawling."

Holding up his hands like Ed Sullivan to quiet the audience, Michael A. said, "Look, guys, I know I've been a beast."

"Infes*tat*ion," Jen said. "Thank *god* my folks aren't around for this, this degradation." Looking at Jack, she said, "I told you he was diseased."

"Real low blow, Cuz," Jack said. "Downright dadblamed dirty-filthy-low."

Michael A. now looked at Taj for sympathy, pity, anything, but all he got was two thumbs down.

"You're an MCP," Natasha said, "I don't know what I saw in you—we're through."

"Surely you jest"—desperation in his voice—"no more Mex-amerileb? What is this—PMS?"

"What's 'PMS'?" Jack said, so Jen leaned over to whisper in his ear. "Say whut?" said Jack. So Jen whispered some more and he said, "Oh, I getcha."

Natasha said, "You no doubt gave me the crabs, you two-timing creep."

"Who among us is perfect?" Spreading his arms to plead his case.

"Cuz, that pose just makes you look like a mule-mouthed politician."

"You've exposed us to a social disease," Jen said.

"V.D.," Michael A. said, nodding, agreeing. "The gift that keeps on giving. But crabs are nothing. With all the free love around these days there's worse to come, worse than syphilis I bet."

Natasha now picked up the carton of Cole slaw and dumped it on his head.

"Thanks for letting me experience woman's inhumanity to man, darlin'."

Natasha now took his Dixie cup and dumped Big Red over his head.

"My oh my, what a complex karma we're developing, darlin'."

Natasha said, "We are hereby convening a house meeting."

"What on earth for, darlin'?"

"A question of hygiene—and never call me darlin' again, scum bucket."

"Love will find a way, ducks, I just know it will." Then: "I still say we need a name for the band. Now I like Kickass Kids—anyone else got a suggestion?"

Natasha said to everyone, "What do we do about this?"

Michael A. said, "Really, if we all just follow the directions on the bottle …" Then stifled himself, wilted once more before that withering white hot glare. "Sorry, dar—, uh, oops …me and my big mouth."

Scowling, Natasha said to the others, "In view of recent findings I'm pissed."

Michael A. said. "My pride and dignity are the integrity that holds my honor together. As Nacho says, 'Live a little each day or die a little each day, the—'"

"Today'd be good," Natasha said. "By your own hand would be best."

"The sooner the better," Jen said, giving Michael A. a white hot death glare.

# CHAPTER NINETEEN

Taj had started using the downstairs bathroom when he grew tired of sharing a bath with Natasha and Michael A. The situation had been especially peevish in the mornings because their three schedules conflicted. And Michael A.'s pattern of dynamic tension only exacerbated the conflict. "Raise the lid, Natasha," he would say and this was right away followed by "Siddown, creepo—no mess, no fuss that way." Taj had grown tired, too, of Michael A.'s infantile graffiti; he scrawled limericks in black Marks-A-Lots on the bathroom walls, each limerick starting with *Here I sit and spit*. It did not help that he never returned the Marks-A-Lots.

Thus, Taj had soon taken the downstairs bath for himself.

That had been the idea, anyway.

But from the very first he had been hearing a woman's voice crooning songs from within the north wall of the bathroom. A surprisingly good voice, too, singing "I Know You, Rider," "House of the Rising Sun" and "Gimme Some Lovin'."

So on Tuesday, April 23, when students at New York City's Columbia University occupied the administration building to protest the Vietnam War, Taj wrote on the 'Z' Room wall *Be realistic— demand the impossible!*

And decided he would do just that.

Thus, that same afternoon Taj walked out of the Student Union Building, gave a salute of solidarity to Natasha and her fellow members of Students for a Democratic Society as they fired up the students about the Columbia takeover, and decided on the way home to go up into the attic in order to learn more about the chimney he had discovered on the roof. When lying on his twin mattress he had seen a trap door in the ceiling of his bedroom. So by folding his mattress and placing it atop his overturned bass drum as a boost, he could reach up and push open the trap door. Next he took the rope ladder he used to get up to the roof and hooked it to an eave to pull himself up into the attic. There, amidst the heat and dust, he saw the chimney passing down through the attic's center. After pausing briefly to note stacks of yellowed sheet music of old songs from the 200 West 19th Street's days as the Waterloo Music Academy, Taj was making his way to the chimney via the eaves, trying not to fall through his bedroom ceiling. This was when he spotted a small wooden box. Once Taj had reached it he saw it was a most unusual box, one with copper fittings.

A three lock box.

. . .

When Cool Breeze came to the back door Michael A.'s greeting was "*Welll!* If it ain't *The Man From Uncle.* What's your story, morning glory?"

But Cool Breeze would not come in the house. Instead, he whispered something in Michael A.'s ear that drained the blood from his face. Finally, Michael A. got it together enough to point at the driveway and Cool Breeze went out to the street, drove his pink 1956 Cadillac into the driveway and parked it as out of sight as possible. Michael A. then came over to Cool Breeze, saying:

"You can stay downstairs if you want."

Cool Breeze shook his head. "*Nunh*-uhhh, *nooo* ghost for company."

"Oh?...You know about the ghost?"

"Hell yeah I do. This house is, as my momma'n granmomma say, 'hainted.' See, they say that back in World War I there was a work-ing lady name of Mona in this house of ill repute an' when she got jilted by some soldier, that was all she wrote—woman hung herself. Went up to the roof, put a rope around her neck, tied it off to the chimney an' jumped in—25, 30 feet down to the fireplace. Fall took her head right off. They found her body on the floor, her head on her belly—*awww*ful sight, man. An' ever since then this house been hainted. When none of the other working' gals would live here, the place become a frat house—but not for long. Frats couldn't take no haint neither. At night Mona'd commence ta moanin'n groanin'an' some even said they seen her head floatin' around. Next it was the Music Academy so nobody around at night. Now Tunoose bought it'n let you honkies move in." Cool Breeze grinned. "How you likin' it so far, Mister Hoochie Coochie Man? Got voodoo vibes, do it?"

Michael A.'s reply was, "What fireplace?"

# CHAPTER TWENTY

At Taj's suggestion they decided to renew the bond cracked by Michael A.'s crabs faux pas by working on, "One World, One Planet", the new song that Taj and Jack had begun piecing together the day Dr. Martin Luther King was murdered. What better way to renew a bond, they thought, than creating a sentiment that Dr. King had helped put together, a piece of originality they could keep in their hearts and hear in their heads, feel in their feet. Something they could share with others.

Besides, a song of their own made them want to name the band.

So that afternoon, after Taj had whipped up his latest batch of couscous and placed it well out of the reach of Wiley and Beep Beep, he and Jen and Natasha came into the dining room. Jack and Michael A. were watching *The Uncle Jay Show*. A *Road Runner* cartoon was on, the one where Wile E. Coyote chases Beep Beep off a cliff only to find himself hanging helplessly in the air for a moment before succumbing to the big fall to Earth. Jen walked over in front of them to turn off the Stromberg Carlson then faced Michael A. with the same dead eyes stare she had been giving him ever since the crabs calamity had hit the fan.

"I'm not breaking any house rules," Michael A. said, getting defensive. "I got skivvies on, Fruit of the Loon baby blue boxers—wanta see?"

"I see them all too well. They're hanging out of your cutoffs—*yeccch!*"

Natasha said, "This is not about Rule Number Three."

"What then?" Michael A. said, frowning briefly before his eyes popped wide open with a case of The Fear. "Oh no, it's not about the band, is it?"

"As it so happens, it is," Jen said.

Michael A. now said in a pitiful tone of voice, "Ohhh mannn. You can't kick me out, guys." Turning to Jack, he said, "Cuz, please, we're family."

Jack looked at Jen and said, "What's up?"

"If we're gonna have a party, we need a name for the band."

"Right. Party. Our coming out party." Michael A. said, his relief obvious.

Jack said, "When is it? Our party?"

"After finals," Natasha said.

"Saturday night, June 1st looks good," Jen said. Then: "Is that good for you, Jack? A little get-together? Play some tunes for people we know … little pity party for you after you've officially flunked out?"

"I'm not gonna flunk out, Jen."

"Right," Michael A. said. "Nobody here's flunking out, it can't happen here." Then: "So we need a name for the band. Got to have something to put on the handbills, advertising, word of mouth an' all like that. Now me, personally, I like The Kickass Kids—anybody else go for that?" Getting zilch for support, he said, "Okay, who else has a suggestion?"

Taj held up his white vinyl clipboard. On it was written *The Bookies*.

"Right," Michael A. said. "The Bookies. On accounta you guys work at the library, sure. But not all of us work there so—"

"I doubt you even know where the library is," Jen said.

Trying to be nice, Michael A. only said, "Any other suggestions?"

Taj held up his white vinyl clipboard again. *Red Hot Warriors*.

Jen said, "Twilight Freeway."

"Porch Lizards," Jack said. "Or Psychedelic Porch Lizards."

*Children of the Red Crescent* was now on Taj's white vinyl clipboard.

"Psychedelic Whomp Dogs," Jack said.

"So many choices, so many," Michael A. said then looked at Natasha. "Anything from you, my brooding beauty? How do you feel about The Kickass Kids? Or The Kickass Kats? They do anything for ya?"

Two thumbs down was Natasha's reply.

In the end, though, Natasha came up with a suggestion for a band name, one that everybody but Michael A. went for right away. But Natasha's withering white hot death glare kept boring into Michael A. until he caved in.

So Dixie cups were raised high to The Psychedelic Crabs.

. . .

After crabs invaded the 19th Street house privacy meant a closed door. Due to the crabs calamity all towels and bed sheets had been washed, though Michael A. made a big production of holding onto the sheets he had shared with Natasha. In fact, he declared he would never wash said sheets until she came back to him.

"Those sheets are all I have left of my only ever darl—uh, brooding beauty."

Natasha's reply was, "Go ahead'n reek in your self-loathing pity party all you want, drama queen. Now"—thrusting her hand out—"gimme 'em."

So Michael A. gave up the sheets. Though he did hold on for dear life when Jen and Natasha insisted he surrender his Fruit of the Looms to an incinerator.

"Have it your way, ladies. It just means I'm goin' commando—nothin' between me'n my boys an' the outside world but my cutoffs."

"Rule Number Three," Natasha said, "Underwear for women optional, required for men."

. . .

Friday, April 26, 1968, the nuclear weapon "Boxcar" was detonated in Nevada.

. . .

Tuesday, April 30, at the administration's request police stormed Columbia University's occupied buildings and removed the protesters within.

. . .

Friday, May 3, North Vietnamese and United States delegations agreed to open peace talks in Paris. That evening in Batts Hall Auditorium Purple People Eater Productions showed *Reflections in a Crystal Eye* with Elizabeth Taylor, Marlon Brando, Brian Keith, Julie Harris and Robert Forster. The profit was $422.

. . .

Monday, May 6, "Bloody Monday" took place in Paris, France. Five thousand students battled with riot police using gas grenades.

. . .

Friday, May 10, in Batts Hall Auditorium Purple People Eater Productions showed *The Graduate* with Dustin Hoffman, Anne Bancroft and Katherine Ross. Profit: $486. The next morning the debt to Strait Music Company was settled.

. . .

Saturday night, May 11, Natasha and Jen went to Hyde Park Recreation club. They walked up to a vacant table, selected cue sticks and shot a game of Eight Ball as the patrons ogled "the foxy hippie chicks" and engaged in some locker room humor with cat calls of "cute keester" and "pert cans, nice racks." When done, Jen and Natasha walked out with style like the liberated women they were.

. . .

May 12, Mother's day, Jack and Jen drove in the Fitty Six to Greenwood Cemetery off White Settlement Road in Fort Worth. Jen placed Indian Paint wildflowers on her parents' graves then, with Jack on guitar, stood between their head stones and sang the most haunting rendition of "I Know You Rider" Jack could imagine.

Jen did not shed a tear, but Jack did.

. . .

Also on Mother's Day Cool Breeze picked the locks on the three
lock box. Taj paid him then took the box and the last of a pint
of Homemade Vanilla Blue Bell Ice cream to the roof. There,
surrounded by the kittens while they lapped up the ice cream, he
opened the box to discover a stack of letters and a telegram, all of
these communications wrapped with a purple ribbon. For over an
hour he read these handwritten letters, each and every one having
been written in France during World War I by an American Expe-
ditionary Force soldier named Abe and mailed to 200 West 19th
Street. All of Abe's letters began "My dearest, darling Mona." More
than once Abe mentioned how glad he was to get in this "scrape,"
which, to Taj, was a sign of how much the times had changed. In
each letter Abe mentioned how much he loved Mona, wanted to
marry her and take her away from 200 West 19th Street so they
could start a new life together.

The telegram in the three lock box was from the Department of
the Army. It said that Abe had been killed in action.

Like the letters, the telegram was addressed to Miss Mona
Devine, 200 West 19th Street, Austin, Texas.

Taj was moved by the letters. Something his mother had always
told him kept crossing his mind. "My special child," she would say,
"nobody hears what you don't say." He tried to stop feeling blue by
watching the kittens. By now Taj knew that all the kittens were fe-
males. He named the white one Hannah and the four calicos Hazel,
Dot, Persia and Phoebe. They had been young enough to need his
help when he first heard them mewing beneath the front steps as he
went to pick up the newspaper. Later, when he saw the cat that had
chased the red laser spot into Kilroy dead on the street, run over, he
knew it was their mother. So Taj had brought her litter up to the
roof and made a home for them by lining one of Big John's fruit
crates with sheet music. He fed and watered and loved the kittens.
When they got big enough to meander he tried to teach them to

use the nearest oak's tree limbs to climb down to the ground. But only Hannah would do it.

It would be Hannah who led him to Mona.

Feeling better, Taj next had to suppress a mischievous smile as he thought back a few months when Michael A., bags under his eyes and fear in his voice, had described his first night in the house. How Michael A. had gone downstairs his first night in the 19th Street house and seen that his bedroom had been invaded. Everything already been arranged, bed made, his bathroom tidy, his Marlon Brando, James Dean and Che Guevara posters on the wall, his Judy Jetson lunch box and lava lamp set beside his water bed.

Just thinking of his prank made Taj grin with glee.

. . .

May 16 was a day the Students for a Democratic Society declared to be "Gentle Thursday." Flowers were passed around outside the Union on the West Mall, a band called Texas Pacific played the blues and leftist political speeches were given in which demands were made of the University's administration. Even some political theatre was performed: first, Michael A. burned his draft card then skedaddled before the campus cops could nab him. Next Natasha pulled out a pink bra and set it on fire before allowing herself to be led away by the same cops. Natasha resisted not a bit. In honor of Dr. Martin Luther King she bit her tongue and remained nonviolent. She did get her licks in vocally, though, by yelling an anti war slogan: "Pull out, Nixon—like your father should've done!" Then she followed this up with "We are the people our parents warned us about." As she was being led away someone from within the crowd who sounded an awful lot like Michael A. yelled:

"Hey, *pig!* Just what're the charges against that beautiful martyr to freedom, justice and the American Way?"

"Indecent exposure, starting an unauthorized fire on campus," a cop said.

"Don't worry, dar—er, martyr woman, I'll write you every day," said the voice in the crowd.

But Natasha was not in the clink long. She was promptly sprung by Uncle Tunoose's bail bondsman. That evening she was in the dining room of the 19th Street house sitting at the head of the church-door-turned-dining-room-table and watching the Channel 7 Evening News. As news anchor Neal Spelce showed footage of Natasha burning the bra, Michael A. said:

"Dayum! Look at my brooding beauty doin' that good deed for her gender."

Then Jack said, "Hey, Jen, isn't that's your front-end loader?"

"Yes, it is," Jen said, touch of pride in her voice.

Michael A. winked at Jack and said, "Are ya gonna miss that big ol' over-the-shoulder-boulder-holder, Cuz?"

"Not a lick—that thing's a crime against Mother Nature."

"It's a symbol of the system's violation of women's rights," Natasha said.

"That's my girl!" Michael A. said, but getting nothing from Natasha, he sighed and said, "I gotta question, how come it's 'bra' if it's 'panties'?"

"Absurd juxtaposition," Jack said.

. . .

Friday afternoon, May 17, Michael A. went out the back door of the 19th Street house and into the driveway. There Cool Breeze was leaning against the trunk of a 1958 Ford Fairlane that he had just maneuvered into the driveway between a VW bug and a Renault. He had done so because Cool Breeze's new business venture was parking students' vehicles in the driveway for 25 cents an hour. He tried to up his income more by peddling record albums and booze he kept in the trunk of his 1956 pink Cadillac. But when Michael A. showed up Cool Breeze was getting an earful from Jen. She was complaining about the legality, morality and coolness of this new 19th Street enter-prise—until Cool Breeze shut her up by taking from the Caddy's trunk the just out debut album of Big Brother and the Holding Company. As Jen walked off studying the album cover, entranced by her bribe, Cool Breeze bit into the toothpick in the corner of his mouth and said:

119

"Man oh man, but that gal's one high-powered piece a energy, ain't she?"

"You got that right," Michael A. said.

"That's some frown that gal's got—don't let it bite you in the ass."

"Check," Michael A. said and went on as to why he had come out to the driveway to see Cool Breeze. "Knowing full well that nothing lasts forever, I, the intrepid ethereal drifter, am telling you, Cool Breeze, right here and now that I shall accede to my uncle's wishes and fly off into the face of adversity."

"Do tell? And what you gonna use for wings, Mister Hoochie Coochie Man?"

"Eighty pounds of balls hanging offa Mexamerileb sausage. See, I'm doin' it for my girl. I wanta buy the 19th Street house for Natasha."

"You serious, huh?"

"Very. And tell my uncle that I can be bought but not owned."

"Well alrighty then, eighty pounds it is," Cool Breeze said, grinning around the toothpick in the corner of his mouth. "'Bout time you got wise an' me an' your uncle got well." Then, taking out a string of car keys, Cool Breeze went over to the 1958 Ford Fairlane he had just parked and opened its trunk. "Yeah," he said, "this oughta do for your eighty pounds—I be back d'rectly."

Later, Michael A. walked down to Clyde Campbell's Men's Shop on the southwest corner of the Drag and 24th Street and bought a blue Gant sports shirt, L.L. Bean chinos, Gold Cup navy socks and a pair of brown Bass Weejuns.

. . .

Friday evening, May 17, in Batts Hall Auditorium Purple People Eater Productions showed *The Big Sleep* starring Humphrey Bogart and Lauren Bacall. At an admission price of $1.25 a head they made $386. Michael A. did not work the door as usual—Jack did—because Michael A. was packing eighty pounds of one-pound bricks of pot into a pair of Jen's olive green Samsonite suitcases.

120

Saturday morning, May 18, Cool Breeze gave Michael A. a phone number to memorize then put Jen's olive green Samsonite suitcases into a Yellow Cab that took the now intrepid ethereal drifter to Mueller Airport off Manor Road. Using the name K.G. Pilgrim, Michael A. later flew on Braniff Airlines to Dallas Love Field where he caught a connecting American Airlines flight to Boston's Logan International Airport. Upon arrival he dialed the memorized number from a pay phone. Next he took a cab to a bar on Beacon Hill called The Bull & Finch. There, as soon as the two Samsonite suitcases were unloaded from the cab's trunk, a guy named Mugsy pulled up in a black Lincoln Continental with a bumper sticker saying *Mafia staff car, keepa you hands off.* The deal was done in the an alley: Mugsy opened the trunk of the Continental and weighed the "goods" on an Ohaus scale inside. Michael A. was then paid off in one-hundred-dollar bills. A cab took Michael A. and the $16 grand from Mugsy to the Hilton Hotel where he got a sixth floor room with an open window. There was nothing to do, so he tried two firsts in his life: using room service to order corn beef hash. He then watched TV, paranoid as all get-out about being robbed, busted or both.

Between the paranoia, the open window's street noise and the racket in the hallway he did not sleep a wink that night.

In the morning he had another first—something called a "bagel"—and checked out, got a cab to Logan and caught his flight home to Texas.

He arrived home a wreck, but a happy wreck.

He wished he had brought a change of underwear, though.

. . .

"I know you, rider," Jen said, her hands on the sides of his head, her palms over his ears, her fingers deep in his hair. "Now ride, Cowboy, ride."

"Rock me, baby," he said. "Rock me all night long."

Afterwards, lying next to him, she said, "Are we gonna grow old together?"

121

"Say whut?"

"You heard me."

. . .

Jack was seated alone in the dining room. He was wearing his old maroon and gold Alpine Bucks football jersey—number Sixty Nine—because it covered his pot belly. Jack was watching the credits of *The Life of Riley* and was more than a little hungover from last night's cheap tequila. When Jen came in she had on her perfect smile and looked drop dead beautiful in cutoffs and yellow tank top, her hair now grown down to well below her shoulders. She came up behind Jack and, placing her hands on his shoulders, she leaned forward to rest her chin on his head as she moved her arms down over his chest.

But all she got was a long, chilly silence.

So Jen raised up and just stood there, pretending to watch the Stromberg Carlson TV until, finally, she said, "Fine. What's on next?"

"*Rocky and Bullwinkle.*"

More silence until the titles were done and a commercial for Leif Johnson Ford was running.

"Do you really, really like *Rocky and Bullwinkle*, Jack?"

"Yeah, pretty much. I like the "Fractured Fairy Tales" part best, especially Edward Everett Horton's narration—he was an old timey character actor in the 1930s and did some flicks as Fred Astaire's sidekick."

More silence as Rocky and Bullwinkle and Peabody the dog came on and did their part of the show. Jack alternately read the back of a Cheerios box with Mickey Mantle on the cover and watched the Stromberg Carlson, chuckling intermittently. "They make it like the squirrel's smarter than the moose—do you think that's really the way it is in nature?"

Jen, arms folded across her chest, shrugged and said, "Fiercely independent critter versus a herd animal? Yeah"—another shrug—"I guess so." Next, unfolding her arms and placing her hands on her hips, she said, "Jack, this can't go on."

Sounding tired, Jack said, "How come?"

"You watch wayyy too much TV."

"If I told you why, you'd laugh, you wouldn't believe me."

"I won't laugh and of course I'll believe you."

"Well, see, I never had a TV before and ya get kinda sucked in."

"Ever forward, huh? Or outward. Ben Jack Gage, can't you see you're getting a paunch from all the processed crap and junk food? All those empty calories you're woofing down are no good for you— you know that don't you? You need more roughage in your diet."

"I'm what I eat, am I? Are you testing my willpower, Jen? Is this a test of my sincerity? Why don't you just simmer down'n quit wartin' me? The fact is, up until this semester I mostly ate down on the drag at Hank's or GM Steak House—you know, chicken fried steak, greasy fires, side of iceberg lettuce and tomato for a salad with french dressing." Then: "Look, Jen, I gotta twinge of the misery and—"

"You mean you're hungover. I swear, Jack, tequila's gonna be the death of you. You're getting zits and your teeth are probably rotting. You're being swept away by the tide of temptation via consumerism so much that you're in danger of being caught up in the draft and sent to Vietnam."

"I doubt that, Jen, I really do. They play for keeps in Vietnam and I don't wanta learn how to kill folks, I really don't—and I won't."

"Jack, you're slacking off so much you're gonna flunk out."

"I don't think so but, well, they need guitar players in Canada too." Then: "Hey, I'm fiercely independent is all an' you wouldn't love me if I weren't. But I'm not perfect—I'm no white knight."

"Tell me about it."

"Why you gotta be so dadblamed flippant, Jen?"

"I'm just being me is all. *Me!* The one who's trying to carry you in school—but you're *gonna flunk out!*"

"Bulll! Scho pro maybe—and if that happens, I'll get off it in summer school."

"You got a problem, Jack. You're up all night so much that most nights we're not even sleeping together—we're growing apart."

123

"We are, huh? We're going through some changes, sure, but we just gotta pull together. Like Nacho says: "Caca pasa, chachalaca.""

"Sounds like just another circumcised idea. What about our pact? 'We are three: you, me and *us*. We fight for you, we fight for me, we fight for *us*. We don't live 'for' each other, we live 'within' each other.'" Her voice pleading now as she said, "Jaaack, won't you fight for us just a little?"

"I *am*, Jen, I am. But I'm against appeasement. You're just a spoiled city girl who's pouting about not getting her way."

"I'm not pouting, I'm fighting for *us*."

"Well, so am I but I gotta be me right now in my life—it's important. I'm into something with the music—let me shoot my lightning through the sky, will ya?"

"Fine—but you're losing sight of *us*."

"Some days, Jen, *us* is all I think about."

"*Bull!*"

"Well, if you ain't the genuine article, Jen. You look an' feel better'n any lady I've ever been around an' I adore you but, like I keep telling you, I'm fiercely independent." Then Jack sighed and said, "We knew we were going to have conflicts, right? This'll keep, Jen—save it for finals."

"But it *won't* keep, Jack. If you keep cutting class Uncle Sam's gonna ship your cute patoot off to the Republic of South Vietnam toute suite, bub."

Jack grinned. "Awww now, do I really have a cute patoot?"

In that moment there came a gentle rapping at front door that gave a forlorn Jen the chance to get away, at least let the roaring in her ears die down. But, when she saw though the door's pane of glass who it was, that internal howl did indeed relent. There was such a reversal of her emotions that she broke down and for the first time since her parents' passing she cried. She bawled like a baby.

But those sapphire eyes of hers were not wet with remorse or self-pity.

No, the presence at the front door was bringing Jen sweet tears of joy.

# CHAPTER TWENTY ONE

Nacho said that, "The dead live with us like a dream within a dream … caca pasa, chachalaca. Therefore I do not mind sleeping downstairs.

Nacho took to Taj right away. He particularly liked Taj's vibes, his aura. "Taj and I are simpatico," said Nacho, "we are fellow travelers." Taj liked that. That night and every night after during Nacho's visit the old one and the young one spent time on the roof together. Their conversations were elliptical, but not because Taj lacked a voice . The night Nacho arrived, as Taj's orange Motorola transistor radio was tuned in to Radio KNOW playing the Zombies "Song of the Season," the old Maya daykeeper gestured toward the kittens and said:

"Which is dominant?"

*The white one rules the roost* Taj wrote on his white vinyl clipboard.

"Ah," Nacho said, "of course, the one with a neutral color. You realize that a cat does not care to do anything that is not its own idea, yes?"

Taj smiled and wrote *Ghosts too.*

Nacho said, "Ah, you *do* get the idea, don't you?" When Taj nodded, Nacho said, "Most ideas rise to the surface, there to burst and somehow impart their meaning, have their say, whether we understand them or not."

Taj wrote *Nonetheless, one must note their import and pay attention, give respect, lest ideas be lost for life is change, no? Ever forward.*

Nacho said, "It is good you know to look to the past for lessons and to the future for answers. I suspect you also know it is better to go slow rather than burn with a crackling ambition lest your hungry brain become a crisp."

Taj nodded and wrote *My parents say that sometimes all one needs is a spark and that this spark may lie dormant for years on one's sail through time's sea. Better to be a buzzard aloft than an eagle on a death dive.*

"Yet one must flap his wings, yes?" Nacho said. "Surely one may not desire to glide along on the tide of life while being sustained by a mere dream."

Taj wrote *Wiser to see only a shadow instead of complete darkness.*

There was silence and they listened to Donovan's "Catch the Wind" until Nacho said, "So is your generation like so many others that have come before? Is it on the way to dust again? A glimmer in a blind eye?"

*Less is more. Think big but see petite.*

"The Big Picture," Nacho said, nodding. "Wiser not to search for lions, tigers and elephants for it is the little lives that bring the details to the building blocks."

Nodding his assent, Taj wrote *What it is is what it was is what it shall be.*

They listened to the remainder of "Catch the Wind" while mingling with the kittens who treated them as if they were trees to climb on, limbs to laze upon. Finally Nacho said, "I sense that you can be quite the rascal, yes, Taj?"

Taj shrugged and grinned. As Frank Sinatra's "That's Life" now played on Radio KNOW, his grin devolved into a mischievous smile and he wrote:

*Caca pasa, chachalaca*

. . .

For the May rains that had been predicted by a University meteorology professor to be twice the norm, Taj constructed a shelter for the kittens. Using the chimney as a windbreak to the west, he took an orange crate and roofed and sided it with loose floorboards he had found in the attic. Next he lined the shelter's interior with yellowed sheet music left over from the days of the Music Academy. Everybody but Hannah took to the shelter. Now, near midnight, with

Hannah was stretched out atop the north wall of the chimney, her fluffy white tail hanging down, watching as Taj lubricated the super duper television antenna's motor with machine oil. When Taj saw Hannah quickly redirect her gaze and her fluffy white tail twitch in warning, he turned see Nacho, hear him say:

"It is pointless to look for the answer so much as the question. We are here not because we were asked or of our own volition. Our time here is short, so once one gets a grip on life then one uses it to pull forward. Though it is sufficient to simply sit and wonder, when the sky is starless and we have gone into eclipse and darkness is eating our sun, only the light within will shine away that darkness."

Taj lowered his eyes and reached for the white vinyl clipboard on his belt. Taking his Marks-A-Lot from the pencil protector in his shirt pocket, he wrote:

*We have met the virus and it is us*

Nacho's wrinkled old eyes beamed above the smile on his lips as he looked at Hannah and said, "Here is our ghost—what else, yes?"

Taj did not reply but Hannah stopped twitching her tail.

"Not to worry," Nacho said to her," for I am another like yourself."

"The tail tells the tale," thought Taj.

. . .

Everybody was cramming for finals. Everybody, it seemed, but Michael A. Finals week was Hell Week for all but him, who was drinking more and enjoying it less. Thus it was on an afternoon in late May that he and Natasha had it out. Their row began in the kitchen then spilled over into the dining room. Since Michael A.'s return from Boston, from Connelly's Florist a dozen yellow roses had arrived daily for Natasha. Today's delivery made ten red Folger's coffee cans filled with yellow roses on the church-door-turned-dining-room-table. But Natasha was in a surly mood because SDS faculty adviser Larry Caroline had been fired from his position in the Philosophy Department and she had just had crashed and burned on her poly sci final.

"Having flowers killed so as to court me won't win me back," she said to Michael A. as he watered the roses. "You still do not know me." Then she stormed off to her bedroom, combat boots stomping loudly across the oak floor.

Michael A. then walked zombie-like back into the kitchen and went on a massive fooder: he dumped a family size box of Captain Crunch into a mixing bowl and drowned it with Superior Dairies Homogenized Milk. Into the dining room he went and sat in front of the Stromberg Carlson TV and commenced to devour this Captain Crunch concoction. When done gobbling it down, he went to the kitchen pantry and came out with a paper plate piled high with Hostess Cupcakes and Twinkies, Oreo Crème Sandwiches and Lay's Potato Chips. Once sated, he washed it all down with two quarts of 39-cent Old Milwaukee beer. He did not even watch TV. When Natasha came out to give him another piece of her mind, he burped out a belch that would stun an elephant and before she could get a word out said:

"Let's go subjunctive—how would you see it if you were me?"

"*Pig!*" Natasha said then proceeded to go bonkers, bananas, ballistic and more. First she kicked at him with a combat boot but failed to connect with the Mexamerileb family jewels. Then from the church-door-turned-dining-room-table she grabbed Folger's cans, hurling them at Michael A. who, slurring, yelled at her:

"Why doncha come here an' play the slobber blues on this ol' Mexamerileb meat whistle, *darrrlin*?"

"*PIG!*"

"C'mon an' gobble ma goober, why doncha? Bite me!"

"*PIG!*"

"Gnaw an' slurp my privates! Slap'n' tickle 'em! Bump uglies! Horizontal mambo—less go into da Den a 'Niquity an' make the water bed boil."

"*PIG!*"

"Thass for me to know an' you to fine out. Show me yours an' I'll show ya mine. Give it the old college try—could be providential!"

Natasha said, "House Rule Number Two—ya leave it ya lose it."

"I didn't leave it, I strayed."

"In order for there to be a depolarization of the sexes there must be an upheaval of machismo masculinity—so move over, *we're* takin over."

"Wait, who's takin' over?"

"Women, *PIG!*"

Michael A. took a deep breath of acquiescence, a profound sadness now in his eyes that dropped over his face like the executioner's black hood. Staggering off to one side, he said, "So thass it. What we had is … dead?"

"It's not dead, pig. It's like it was never even born."

. . .

The 19th Street and University kids went to Eeyore's Birthday Party in Eastwoods Park not too far from J. Frank Dobie's white frame home. Michael A. was uptight, keyed up and more than a tad wasted, his voice often rising, intense because he had ducked into Taj's room and availed himself of one of Taj's peyote buds for some visionary enlightenment. Having administered this barfy sacrament with a large bowl of Blue Bell Homemade Vanilla Ice Cream, Michael A.'s eyes turned into pinpoints and his aura became a red devil's halo. Right now he was telling all within earshot that he was mad as hell and was not going to take it anymore. He was further making an ass of himself by ogling all the women.

"Hear ye, hear ye, lesbian terrorists! The perfect woman in these trying times is three feet tall and her teeth fold back an' she's got a flat head for a guy to sit his beer on." Then, in a maudlin tone of voice: "Suddenly she comes into a guy's life an' doses you with that crazy little thing called love."

Though the scents of Shalimar, Aqua Velva and pot smoke were melding in the spring air among the partying coveys of coeds and underclassmen, grad students, faculty and staff spread out on the green grass, Michael A. suddenly got a whiff of a different scent.

129

"Do you douche with Lavoris, darlin'?" Saying this as he walked up to a doe-eyed honey of a coed. "You should—it does wonders for your sex life."

The coed promptly obeyed her instincts—and daddy's advice—and fled.

Heads were turning now, eyes were flitting, whispers were hissing in the ears of bobble headed androids and Coppertone airheads from the frat set.

"Farm out," one frat said. "That guy's solid gone on something."

"It's not 'farm out'," another frat said, "it's 'far out'."

"Oh," said the first one.

"It could be 'full on right on and groovy'," said another.

"There ain't no life nowhere," Michael A. said to a bleached blonde. "Avoid my horny stare lest you lust for my seed an' your tummy be filled with something other than Dirty Martin's cheeseburgers'n fries, Threadgill's chicken fried steak'n Der Weinersnitzel dogs for I'm the god of hellfire an' I bring you … crabs!"

"We're at war, nut job," said a guy in a R.O.T.C. uniform.

"Loose lips sink ships," Michael A. fired right back. "But we who stand and wait still serve." Next he held up his hands as if to command attention like a snake oil salesman on Main Street USA and said, "Dristan decongestant and Arid Extra Dry, Katie Winter's Ice Blue Secret with a hint of clap, Super Animist an' Bayer Aspirin, Geritol, Midol and Tampons an' Trojans, Spraynet'n Vitalis an' Vick's Vaporous—getcha blue eyes an' turned up noses above high school braces sprayed right here, folks … gotta discount special on circumcised ideas this lovely afternoon, yes indeedy dooo!" Then he said to himself:

"Mannn, ohhh, mannn, but this venting is *goood!*"

Next, though, he heard a familiar female voice hissing in his ear, saying: "Why do women love to hate you, pig?"

Recognizing the voice, Michael A. said to himself, "Uh-oh, a feenie from my sordid past—this could get ugly." Then he said to the feenie: "Darlin' Daphne, don't ya understand it's because women want me yet know they can't have me."

"You really believe that?"

"It's the only way that I make it through the night, darlin'—I live with a ghost."

"You belong in a cage."

"Well, before that comes to pass—as it may very well might—I'm gettin' the hell a*wayyy* from *youuu.*" Then he ran off, zigzagging across the green grass like a Keystone Cop, all the while screaming out a ranting review of the scene:

"Homespun hippies, counter-culture individualists rubber-stamped in grunge, hair unkempt an' long yet clean an' blow-dried an' adorned with flowers, head bands an' peace symbol necklaces an' leather fringe, leather bracelets an' Omega watches for high school graduation gifts, beads from Sears, State Farm auto insurance an' stock certificates from daddy, sex talks an' bad vibes from mommy. Twisted frats'n babes in miniskirts an' bell bottom jeans annnd ... ouu, a micro skirt—beware the life-sucking legs on that one, bro."

Suddenly and without warning much less awareness, as he ran past an oak tree he was tripped up by a protruding umbrella, causing him to tumble, become a heap on the grass. Next he was struck repeatedly from behind by a raining flurry of umbrella blows, one blow clobbering him so that he dropped his head to the grass and covered up with his hands, leaving his ass sticking high up in the air like an ostrich with its head in the sand. After three umbrella blows to the rump, it ended. Uncovering, he raised his head to peek out, say to the air around him:

"Daphne?"

"And Natasha and Lenore," he heard Jack say as he reached down to give Michael A. a hand up.

"Oh god, god, god, now they're running in a pack," Michael A. said, his voice a raspy echo of itself. "I'm a dead man. I've been under a great strain lately—too much dynamic tension—and, on top of that, hell hath no fury like a woman scorned."

"Not scorned," he heard Jen say behind him. "Be*tray*ed!"

· · ·

Cool Breeze took off his cheesy fedora to wipe the sweat from his brow and lean on his shovel and say, "White kids from the burbs don't know doodly about the Earth and what it can do for you." Cool Breeze was on the west side of house the morning after Eeyore's Birthday Party. Natasha had just left to slice cantaloupe and watermelon for breakfast after tossing hacked up yellow roses into the garden. Cool Breeze now nodded approvingly at the recycling of the hacked up yellow roses and said, "Now that'll make good mulch—uh-huh, sure enough will."

Cool Breeze, Jack, Taj and Nacho were now planting a garden of corn with beans, black-eyed peas and squash planned to be grown later beneath the corn. Jen was mostly watching and Michael A. was seated on the ground, bemoaning his hangover, completely unaware that the brown bag beside him held fertilizer de Wiley and Beep Beep.

"Take, take, take from the planet, never give, yeah, that what kids from the burbs do," Cool Breeze said as he sowed. "Ain't this spot deee-vine for a garden what with all this dog poop for fertilizer and"—looking at Michael A.—"*fresh* yellow flowers for mulch? Say there, Mr. Hoochie Coochie man, you reckon those Connelly Florist folks mind if we borrow their water hose to water?"

"Been known to happen," Michael A. said, voice low, sounding near death.

"By the by, y'all, I do dang fine on conga an' I be happy to jam withya."

Jen said, "You're on, Cool Breeze."

Jack said, "And you're welcome to sit in on flute, Nacho."

Whereupon Nacho reached into his colorfully woven Maya rucksack and pulled out his wooden flute to do a brief run on it while dancing a Maya jig.

# CHAPTER TWENTY TWO

For today's dawning, Nacho seemed particularly solemn and full of resolve. He and Taj stood on the roof watching a pink dawning being bisected by a streak of jet-plane's chem trail of vapor moving from east to west. Hannah was on the nearest limb of the oak tree, tail twitching, her green eyes alert. Like the kittens in the orange crate, she was watching Taj and Nacho with calm acceptance. Venus—in its aspect as Lord Morningstar—was off to the left of Cambridge Tower. Usually, at 26 million miles away, Venus was the closest planet to Earth but sometimes, Nacho said, Mars was closer when Venus's orbit around the sun took that planet 160 million miles away. Taj had been learning about being a Maya daykeeper from Nacho. Taj now knew that a daykeeper was more than someone who kept the sacred days in the ancient calendars. A daykeeper also knew every point of light in the heavens and was seen as a transcendent human, one who was on a lifelong quest to bring the past into the present so as to light the way forward. Besides being a daykeeper in this life, Taj felt that Nacho had had a past life—maybe as a cat.

· · ·

It was Taj's 21th birthday, June 1, a Saturday. Also the debut of the Psychedelic Crabs at 200 West 19th Street.

Taj came down from the roof as soon as he heard the stress in Michael A.'s voice calling out from the latter's bedroom window:

"Trouble, Taj. We need you, please. Now, Taj, right *now*."

Stepping off the rope ladder a moment later, Taj saw Michael A., Natasha, Jack and Jen standing in his bedroom, their backs to him as they peered in through the door to the bathroom he had once shared with Michael A. and Natasha. The vibe was gloomy, half of Taj's housemates were shaking their heads woefully, the other half sighing deeply. All turned to look at Taj as Michael A. said:

"Bro, we are in deep poopoo."

"Bottomless poopoo," Jen said.

"We're screwed," Natasha said.

"Our goose is cooked," Jack said.

Taj gestured with his hands to ask *What's wrong?*

Michael A. said, "Our guests of honor will not be presentable at this rate."

"We're screwed," Natasha said again.

"Look," Jen said, stepping aside, pointing into the bathroom for Taj to see.

Taj stepped forward to see what was causing such concern.

"The kegs, man," Jack said. "The beer won't be cold for tonight's bash."

Two sixteen-gallon kegs of beer were sitting upright in the bathtub. Going over to them, Taj placed a hand on each. Frowning at their warmth, he, too, shook his head and turned to see all eyes on him seeking some optimism.

"You're the in-house engineer, Taj," Michael A. said.

"You're our secret weapon," Jack said.

"Ya gotta do something, Everyman," Jen said.

"For the people," Natasha.

Taj frowned some more and walked past his housemates into his bedroom. He placed his right hand to his chin in the thinker's pose, left hand propping up his right elbow as he paced back and forth across the room. Soon his eyes brightened and he raised a finger in the air … only to lower it, momentarily crestfallen.

"We're screwed," Natasha said again.

"Too daunting a task, Taj?" asked Michael A.

Taj vigorously shook his head no and resumed his pacing. Soon he again thrust a finger into the air, inspiring a collective intake of breath from the others.

"He's figured it out," Michael A. said.

134

"I told ya he's our secret weapon," Jack said.

"Way to go, Everyman," Jen said.

"Power to the people," Natasha said.

But then Taj's smile went away and he began to frown some more. With a regret-filled shake of his head he resumed pacing.

"Sufferin' succotash," Michael A. said. "Foiled again, still doomed."

"Rats," said Jen.

"Gosh*dawg*-it!" Jack said.

"Crap," Natasha said.

Taj's pacing continued while his housemates gave him pleading looks, those looks weighing on him, almost causing him to succumb to a feeling of failure—until a grin broke across his face. Like Walt Disney's eccentric-genius cartoon character Gyro Gearloose, Taj once more thrust a finger into the air. This time he began nodding, his inventive mind double checking the plan for his bright idea. Lastly, he reached into his pocket and pulled out a key.

"His entry key," Michael A. said, smile of satisfaction on his face.

"To the Engineering Lab," Jen said, nodding, her sapphire eyes beaming.

"Now you're talkin', Taj," Jack said. "Go 'head an' get 'er done, ya hear?"

"*Hallelujah!*" Natasha screamed at the top of her lungs.

. . .

Taj ordered the bathtub to be filled with twelve inches of water then he scurried from his bedroom, through the dining room and kitchen and, still scurrying, went out the back door and down the back steps into the driveway, into the garage. There he threw a leg over Michael A.'s Triumph 650 motorcycle, used the key already in the ignition to shift into the "Start" position then kick-started the motorcycle on the first try. After back peddling his way out of the garage, he turned the Triumph around in the driveway, put in the clutch with his left hand, placed the gear shift Triumph into first gear with his right foot then took off. Soon he was heading north on University: changing gears, downshifting then turning right onto 21th Street at Littlefield Fountain before heading east to Speedway. There he turned left and entered the campus, took Speedway past Gregory Gym, the Petroleum Engineering Building, the East Mall and Chilling Station then Taylor Hall where he turned right onto 24th Street. At the entrance Taj gunned the Triumph over the curb and up onto the sidewalk. Leaving the Triumph's engine running, he bolted up the steps and inside.

Soon he was exiting the building with a cooler holding five pounds of dry ice. He tied the cooler onto the metal rack behind the Triumph's seat and re-mounted the Triumph, put the key in the ignition, shifted into "Start", kick-started the engine and roared off back the way he had come.

Once back in the 19th Street house Taj dumped the five pounds of dry ice into the bathtub then stepped back to see what he had wrought. The dry ice was dancing on the surface of the twelve inches of water he had ordered put into the bathtub and in no time the bathtub was a boiling pot of devil's stew. A CO2 fog began blanketing the bathtub, this fog continuing to rise until it was overflowing the rim of the bathtub and spilling onto the floor—but now the two kegs were submerged within a bubbling liquid.

When the fog had cleared, the dry ice gone, Taj carefully approached the kegs for a touch test: cold yet still not cold enough. Frowning, he looked at the expectant faces of his housemates and shook his head.

"Curses!" he heard Michael A. say. "Foiled again!"

"Double rats," said Jen.

"*Lawsy mercy*," said Jack.

"Momma mia," said Natasha.

But Taj was already embarking on Plan B. He paid no heed to anyone else and again scurried down the stairs, out the back door and onto the Triumph to roar off again, retrace his route to the Engineering Lab. In less than a minute he emerged cradling a two-liter dewer of liquid nitrogen. Michael A. was exiting the can when Taj re-entered in the 19th Street house and as soon as he laid eyes on the dewer marked *Danger! Liquid Nitrogen!*, he back peddled out into the dining room, an "umber horror" expression on his face, his voice quivering when he said:

"Hey, man, isn't liquid nitrogen the stuff you see smoking around the rockets at Cape Canaveral when NASA is about to have a space launch?"

The other housemates gasped and fled into the dining room, but it was a cool Taj who dumped liquid nitrogen into the bathtub. To the astonishment of all, including Taj, a violent explosion of fog ensued and the bathtub now resembled a volcano in eruption stage, complete with a rumbling gurgle coming from down around the kegs. With everybody else in the dining room, Taj closed the bathroom door to seal off the fog in the bathroom then joined his housemates in the dining room. From there they watched the chemical fog begin seeping out from beneath the bathroom door. For ten minutes they watched and waited. As the fog hung low, there was a "Dayum" from Michael A., "Awww rats" from Jen, "Gollleee" from Jack and "We're screwed" from Natasha.

At the end of those ten minutes Taj crept through the remaining fog to open the bathroom door. As it slowly creaked open all saw a pair of frosty kegs standing up in a bathtub whose bottom was encased in two inches of ice. The beer was frozen solid, but that was okay as there was time enough before the party to remedy that. Everybody then gave Taj a victory hug, Michael A. saying:

"Didn't I tellya Taj is a good guy to have liking you?"

# CHAPTER TWENTY THREE

Like Jack said: "Music inspires us, takes us to a higher level."

On the night of Taj's 21st birthday The Psychedelic Crabs made their debut before friends and peers in the living room of 200 West 19th Street. On the front door a hand-scribbled sign said:

*Just slip inside this house*
*No need knockin' if we're a-rockin'*

Daphne and Lenore were there. Jolinda Biggs was there. Main Librarian Lorena McKee Baker and many of her pages were there. Members of the Students for a Democratic Society were there. Fellow travelers and local underground artists Jim Franklin and Gilbert Shelton showed up. Lots of The Psychedelic Crabs' University classmates, old and new, plus many Chuck Wagon folks were there, Gamma Sigs, too. And, to Jen's surprise, her old mentor from Folk Sing, Janis, showed up, now wanting to be called "Pearl."

Thelma and Barney Lou looked worried, however, seeing all the new faces mugging at them in their goldfish bowl.

The Monkey Ward's stereo warmed up the crowd with The Psychedelic Sounds of the Thirteenth Floor Elevators, Big Brother and the Holding Company's debut album, The Conqueroo, Shiva's Head Band. And, due to Austin's heat, the kegs became unfrozen so there was plenty of ice cold beer.

Nacho called it "legendary time."

Michael A. was keyed up, of course. He had a Houston colt .45s baseball cap on his curly head and a T-shirt with a caricature of Edgar Allan Poe on the front—and a pair of cutoffs with a balled-up sock in the crotch. He told Jack the sock was for "Stage presence, the modern cod piece—I hear the Stones do it. Be good for our image, might become my signature look." Michael A.'s dynamic tension then placed a proprietary hand on Natasha's purple silk mini-skirted fanny only to have it slapped away. But Natasha was grinning when she did this, saying:

"War is not the answer, crab boy."

Emboldened, Michael A. said, "Got something for ya."

"Yeah, what is it?"

"Half a foot of Mexamerileb sausage, dar—er, my brooding beauty."

"That little ol' thing again? What do you expect me do with that?"

"Put it between your lovely pillows an' it'll make your dreams come true."

"Yeah?" she said, still teasing. "How good could that be?"

"The maximum success I refuse to guess."

This was when Jen walked up in Tinkerbell cutoffs and a turquoise peasant blouse and said, "What's that you got on your feet, Michael A?"

"Combat boots, darlin', compliments of dear old Captain Dad." Then, winking: "Just in case a guy has to defend himself, you know, duke it out 'cause ya never know with a crowd of dweebs and revolutionaries like this. Sure do hope none of the women here tonight wear me to a frazzle."

Jen grinned and, also kidding, said, "You sure those combat boots are not for fending off Daphne? Or Lenore?... or Mona?"

Michael A. winced but recovered, grinning back at her as he said, "Heyyy, no moans'n groans tonight, okay? May the voice of whatever's within the walls of our hallowed house nail our songs with her woefully sweet tones, be it humming the melody to "I Know You Rider" or whatever."

And then they got down to it. They did their six cover songs—Cream's version of Robert Johnson's "Crossroads," "I Know You Rider," "House of the Rising Sun," the Zombies "Song of the Season," "Gimme Some Lovin," "I Feel Free,"—and, though, they did not exactly hit their stride, they had enough moments to make their guests at the party cut loose a la *le danse terrible,* enough so that the Psychedelic Crabs felt they were moving on with their music.

They played with Michael A. holding his ax by the neck, a shoulder strap over his left shoulder supporting the hollow body Fender, his fingers plucking away at the bass line. Michael A. stood ramrod straight, like an oak tree, his fingers the branches of that tree and foliating notes that were a perfect canopy for the music of the Psychedelic Crabs.

They played with Natasha hovering like a hawk over her Vox Continental, sometimes a soaring hawk when on her harmonica. Up she went, down she went, her shoulders swaying to the rhythm, bending her knees well below the hem of her purple silk mini skirt.

They played with Jen's 'found' voice unrepentently laying it out strong or sweet and true or raspy as any fallen angel's when it needed to be.

They played with Jack in jeans and a Mexican wedding shirt while he teased the frets of his red Gibson Melody Maker so the blues notes bent, squealed from the guitar pick in his right hand. Jack did his best James Dean as naturally as the man himself. He came off as stolid and cool. A sure shooter.

They played with Taj shirtless and in faded European jeans, his wiry body rippling its tight contours—but it was his head that stole the show: without losing a beat he would flick his tongue from his mouth as does a lizard out to snatch a fly from the air around him, Taj's tongue—and only his tongue—seeming to writhe, undulate. The girls in the crowd went wild.

"You're a devil, Taj," Natasha told him between songs.

"A silver-tongue devil," Jen said. "Rock *onnn.*"

And the Psychedelic Crabs played with Cool Breeze and Nacho sitting in whenever they felt like it: two old guys sending out sounds with soul and verve. Cool Breeze was in his cheesy fedora and baggy brown trousers, his unbuttoned Jamaican shirt showing a hairless brown chest beneath a charm necklace of chicken bones—a gift from Nacho to protect him from Mona. Cool Breeze coaxed the

141

congas like he was kneading electric dough, producing a sound as solid as a drum-thumping heartbeat.

Around Nacho's neck was a slingshot carved by the late Granpa Gage. Nacho played wearing his all-white Maya getup and his little Yucatecan fedora on his wise and wispy old head. From his wooden flute Nacho blew melodic sounds that soared through the house like a giant avian.

And The Psychedelic Crabs' harmonizing was seamless. All those hours holding hands in the dark in the White Room paid off. The bands' voices melded together flawlessly in a way that brought the house together, everybody singing along. Jen and "Pearl" even did a duet, sharing the lead vocal on a verse of "I Know You Rider." And when The Psychedelic Crabs finished off their set with "I Feel Free" they marched off to whoops and hollers and enough applause for a lifetime, their right fists clenched and raised fully above their heads, heads bowed low—a power salute to Dr. Martin Luther King. For an encore they did their song, "One World, One Planet" that had been penned by Taj and Jack—and maybe Mona. At its end they went into "Crab Jam", a bluesy instrumental where they just "felt one another"—as Jack put it— a collaboration in which each did a solo.

"We didn't suck like schmucks," Michael A. said afterward.

"Yeaaah!" Natasha and Jack and Jen—and Taj—harmonized.

"We rocked," Jen said

At the end of the party, as Michael A. was leaving with Daphne, the last words on his lips heard by Jack and Jen were, "Now there's an idea." Then Kilroy came up and, talking to Jack but not taking his eyes off Jen, said, "You Psychedelic Crabs rock! Wanta play our place sometime soon?" When Jack shrugged and said, "Sure, I guess," Kilroy said to Jen said, "Do I know you? I don't know you, do I?"

Jen did not answer, just walked off after flashing Kilroy her perfect smile.

# CHAPTER TWENTY FOUR

Finals were over and done with and Jen was on the honor roll while Jack was on scholastic probation. Hoping somehow to appease his lover, on Tuesday, June 4th, after their library shift, Jack said:

"What say we take a spin in the Fitty Six?"

"Oookay," Jen said, wondering what was up.

So they loaded up Wiley and Beep Beep in the Fitty Six, neither Jack nor Jen saying a word about the new dashboard Jesus or anything else: they rode in silence as Radio KNOW played the Beatles' "Strawberry Fields." After parking by Helen M. Kirby Hall, Jack lowered the tailgate for Wiley and Beep Beep and the four of them walked to the Waller Creek grotto where Jack and Jen had bonded.

"What is this?" Jen said. "A stroll down memory lane?"

"It's a return to the beginning."

In the limestone grotto under the oak tree on a bend in the creek Jack and Jen sat on the concrete bench that was a parental memorial honoring a daughter lost to polio. Jen then surprised Jack by handing him her dad's unopened letter from the first mail delivery to 19th Street and University, saying:

"Would you read it for me, please?" Jen said.

Jack took one look and said, "Now's still not the time, Jen."

"I guess it'll keep," she said, relieved, and put it in the back pocket of her cutoffs saying, "'Keep it pure yet simple, respect yourself an' others'—right?"

"'And listen to your heart, remember that nothin's won if it ain't fun.'"

"An' stay away from that tequila," Jen said, saying it 'ta kill ya.'

Thanks to the May rains there was water in the creek now but no flow, just pools and puddles here and there. Looking up at the oak tree—her "wailing tree"—made Jen feel sad, wonder if this might be their last visit here, this place that Janis had turned her on to, where Jen had let it all out without witnesses.

"Jaaack?"

"Whut?"

"We didn't bring our guitars."

"That's because this isn't about music or romance."

Jen frowned a little and said, "Do you still love me?"

"We're still together, aren't we?"

"Not so you'd notice." Then, feeling a freaky déjà vu twinge about her mom and dad's final days of togetherness:"Maybe we should be by ourselves for a while. I've been thinking about getting into loneliness, see if what that's like. I mean, you've been real sweet, Jack, and I like you a lot for it."

"You dumping me, Jen? You gonna stomp on my heart?"

"I don't know. Look, Jack, I didn't' fall in love with you so you'd become a slacker. Your needs have become so … raw, and our karma's not good right now. It seems like we're embarking on another transforming experience, you know, crossing the threshold into another chrysalis."

"Breaking up is 'a stage of being'?"

"Maybe."

"A crossroads?"

"Oh, definitely."

"Where the caterpillar sees the end of the world but the butterfly sees a bold new one?"

"Right." Then, seeing Beep Beep sniffing Wiley's butt, she said, "Stop that, you silly thing."

Jack said, "You can make Beep Beep quit that for now, Jen, but you can't make a dog stop that sort of thing. It's just nature's way." Then: "You've sure picked a fine time to leave me, Jennifer. You say I'm in trouble, so what do you do—you bail on me. Caca pasa, chachalaca. I thought you had more heart. Maybe you're forgetting our pact but I still say 'We are three: you, me and *us*. We fight for you, we fight for me, we fight for *us*. We don't live 'for' each other, we live 'within' each other.' We fight for you, we fight for me, we fight for *us*."

"We *should* fight for *us*. Since I'm kind of used to you, no, I'm not leaving you, not when you talk like that and sound like you're gonna back it up—we're *on*, again, mister. We're on as long as you talk like that. Like you're fighting for me, trying to win my heart—that's the man I love, the man I fight for."

After a taking a deep breath, Jack said, "Do you know what burros are called in the Big Bend country?"

"Nope."

A male is called a jackass—"

"I knew that."

Jack grinned and said, "And a female is a jenny."

Jen grinned, too. She said, "So you'n me are a couple of jack-asses, huh?"

Then that grin dissolved and that face that Jen would not show, the one that no one else but Jack had seen came over her, that adult face that had showed up in the mirror at the outset of puberty—*that* face came over Jen. They had been so caught up in each other's gravity that she felt he deserved to see it, even if he was letting his life slip away at the University. She said:

"Even though we're consenting adults who can act like we're teenage lovers, you know we're gonna have conflicts, don't you?"

"I love you, you love me, we love each other," Jack said. "Ever forward."

"You know, Jack, there are times—and this is one of them—when a girl just wants to be held."

"A guy does too, Jen."

. . .

It was the hottest day of the year, the humidity so sweltering that Taj had gone to the Chuck Wagon for the air-conditioning. Now he was sitting all by himself at their usual table—which felt odd since none of his other housemates were around. In his lap was a book that Natasha had loaned him called *The Lord of the Rings*. Dylan's "Hard Rain's Gonna Fall" was playing on the jukebox, so Taj read the *Daily Texan*. He learned that Andy Warhol had been shot by Valerie Solanis, a struggling writer, actress and radical feminist, and that the U.S. command had announced that American deaths in first six months of 1968 had exceeded 1967's death toll, American deaths in Vietnam having reached 22,951. Taj was reading that inflation at was at 4.3 percent when he heard someone whispering:

"Is Jack here somewhere?"

Taj looked up to see a small, middle-aged woman, a black lace mantilla covering her head. This woman was unsmiling as she looked around the Chuck Wagon before turning back to Taj to say, "My name is Sofia Medina. My son is Miguel Antonio Medina and Jack is my nephew."

Taj frowned to show that he did not understand.

"Perhaps you know Miguel as 'Michael A.'"

Taj then nodded and smiled.

"You are Taj, yes?"

Again Taj nodded and smiled.

"I have a message from my son," Mrs. Medina said, still whispering. "He wishes you and Jack and his other friends in the band to know that he is in custody and might not be back for a while."

Taj's smile fled.

"Not to worry," she said. Then, after a small shrug: "These things happen for, as you know, caca pasa, chachalaca."

And then she left.

· · ·

A short while later the Monkey Ward's stereo was playing Jefferson Airplane's *Surrealistic Pillow* album. Jack sat in one of the straight back chairs at the church-door-turned-dining-table while Jen stood behind him brushing his long hair with her mom's heirloom brush. Both were barefoot and wore white T-shirts and cutoffs.

When Grace Slick finished singing "Feed your head, feed your head" in "White Rabbit," "Jack said to Jen:

"Cuz is MIA. He hasn't been seen since he left the party with Daphne."

"Then it could be"—giggling to show she was kidding—"that he's probably all hacked up into little bitty pieces and in her freezer."

The Airplane's "Plastic Fantastic Lover" now began as Natasha and Taj came into the dining room and sat down at the church-door-turned-dining-room-table. "Sorry to disappoint you, Jen, but Michael A.'s not in Daphne's freezer or anybody else's," Natasha said. "He's in the clink. The pigs grabbed him up." Taj nodding as Natasha said, "At least that's what his mom just told Taj."

"What'd they get him for?" Jen said. "Scalping tickets? Pot? Possession of stolen property? A Connelly's Florist water hose—what?" Then, voice up an octave: "Oh my god—they busted him for burning his draft card, didn't they?"

"Wrong again," Natasha said. "On May 27 the Supreme Court ruled that burning a draft card is free speech. U.S. versus David Paul O'Brien." Then: "We don't know what they got him for or even who *they* are. All his mom said was that he'll be gone for a while."

"No problem," Jen said, "Uncle Tunoose'll have him sprung in no time."

"Nope," Jack said, shaking his head, "Uncle Tunoose can't help him."

"How come?" Natasha said.

"'Cause Uncle Tunoose's not out yet."

"Out?" Jen said.

"Yet?" Natasha said.

"Yep," Jack said. "Cool Breeze says Uncle Tunoose got locked up."

"Do you think Michael A. and Tunoose got busted together?" Jen said.

"Quien sabe?" Jack said.

Taj then stood up, his face with a curious expression on it as he went past the Stromberg Carlson to fix his gaze on the book case that went all the way to the ceiling. He was not looking in on

147

Thelma and Barney Lou but at something new that had been set beside the fishbowl.

"What in the world is that?" Natasha said.

"Who put that there?" Jen said.

"It had to have been Nacho," Jack said.

Taj took out his Marks-A-Lot to write *Or Mona* on his white vinyl clipboard.

That, along with the news about Michael A., brought a long pall of silence into the dining room. For a long time the four of them just stared at the new addition to the book case: a terra cotta statuette with a round base perhaps ten inches in diameter and standing in a circle around the perimeter of this base were six human figurines, each about six inches high, each with its arms stretched out so the hands were touching the shoulders of the figurines beside them. Nobody said a word until *Surrealistic Pillow's last cut* "Plastic Fantastic Lover" ended. The phonograph needle rose, returned to its holder and the Monkey Ward's Airline Stereo shut off. There was more than just silence now. There was a void of disbelief as everyone's gaze remained fixed on the statuette. Finally, Jack said:

"All the mouths on those terra cotta folks are open."

"They're singing," Jen said.

"They're harmonizing," said Natasha.

"Just like us," Jen said as Taj began to write with his Marks-A-Lot again before holding up his white vinyl clipboard for all to see:

*But who is the sixth?*

. . .

Now they were four in the flesh, not five, but those four could still feel the presence of Michael A. He had been gone since the party. No one had seen hide nor tail of him since he had walked out the door with Daphne. Yet he was somehow still there same as Miss Mona Devine. It was as if in his absence Michael A. was using dynamic tension on them, still being a stinker.

"Absurd juxtaposition's what it is," Jack said.

"And that's the way it is, June 4, 1968," Jen said.

"The revolution will not be televised," Natasha said. Then shrugged and said, "And if it is, the first thing we do is kill all the lawyers."

Taj wiped off his white vinyl clipboard and wrote *Then we eat their livers.*

"Easy there, Everyman," Jen said.

Jack said, "Looks like we're short a bass player."

"Meaning we're at another crossroads," Jen said.

"Yeah," Natasha said, "and it's called 19th and University." Then she sneered and said, "I still say they won't name a street after Martin Luther King."

"Well, if they do," Jen said, "it'll be providential." Then, looking at Jack: "And if you can just stay in school, Mr. Ben Jack Cage, once Bobby Kennedy wins the California primary tonight and then goes on to win the presidency all this Vietnam mess and a lot of our problems will be history."

"Yes, ma'am."

. . .

*Tres said, "So what happened to Michael A.?"*

*"The Big Wind got him."*

*"He was drafted?"*

*"Yes. See, he never enrolled in school and they finally found him through his mother—she thought the military would do him good so she turned him in."*

*"Wow ... but Natasha was wrong, wasn't she, Gram? The City of Austin did name a street after Martin Luther King, didn't they?"*

*"Yes, they did. 19th Street became Martin Luther King Boulevard."*

*"And Robert F. Kennedy was shot and killed the next day, right? And it was the house that brought you all together then the band and its music forged the bond?"*

*"Pretty much. Whatever, it was a humbling yet revealing and rewarding experience. There's more to tell about The Psychedelic Crabs, of course. We'd gone from being clean cut college kids to being longhaired*

*hippies in a rock band. We saw the planet as a whole world, not fenced off by man-made borders."*

*"Back then a guy could die for his country but he couldn't vote," Tres said.*

*"Yeah, but a lot of us were gonna vote back in 1968," Jen said, "You'd durn best believe that we wanted to make a difference."*

*Tres now looked over the photos again. He frowned at one for a while before handing it to Jen, saying, "So tell me who's who in this photo, Gram. It seems different than the others."*

*"Ahhh, well," Jen said, putting on her granny glasses to take a look. "Let's see now ... this one was taken when we were all on the faded red couch that had the American flag on the wall above it ... and on the left is me then Jack, Michael A., Natasha, Taj and, wait ... oh my ... Mona?"*

# ACKNOWLEDGEMENTS

For being there and/or remembering (in alphabetical order),
Barbara Sanborn, Carl Clark (deceased), Dave Moran (deceased),
Dickie Ancell, Dr. Joe Kruppa, Dr. Pat Kruppa, Gail Savage,
Gary Oliver, James McCreary, Patrick Urh. With  special thanks
to Alice Sparks, our interminable word processor
... and to SJ Barba.

www.ingramcontent.com/pod-product-compliance
Lightning Source LLC
Chambersburg PA
CBHW052009240626
47153CB00008B/2802